D0350913

touched

Also by Joanna Briscoe

Mothers & Other Lovers
Skin
Sleep With Me
You

Joanna
Briscoe
touched

HAMMER™
AN EXCLUSIVE MEDIA COMPANY

Published by Arrow Books in association with Hammer 2014

3 5 7 9 10 8 6 4 2

First published in Great Britain in 2014 by
Arrow Books in association with Hammer
Random House, 20 Vauxhall Bridge Road,
London SW1V 2SA

www.randomhouse.co.uk

Addresses for companies within The Random House Group Limited can be found at:
www.randomhouse.co.uk/offices.htm

The Random House Group Limited Reg. No. 954009

A CIP catalogue record for this book
is available from the British Library

ISBN 9780099590828

The Random House Group Limited supports the Forest Stewardship Council®
(FSC®), the leading international forest-certification organisation. Our books carrying
the FSC label are printed on FSC®-certified paper. FSC is the only
forest-certification scheme supported by the leading environmental
organisations, including Greenpeace. Our paper procurement policy can be
found at www.randomhouse.co.uk/environment

Typeset in 13.5/16 pt Centaur MT by Palimpsest Book Production Limited,
Falkirk, Stirlingshire
Printed and bound by CPI Group (UK) Ltd, Croydon, CR0 4YY

For Theodore
with appreciation and much love

ACKNOWLEDGEMENTS

With many thanks to Laura Astin, Jennifer Bates, Tim Bates, Laura Bishop, Carol Briscoe, Michele Camarda, Mary Chamberlain, Gabrielle Dalton, Helen Healy, Catherine Heaney, Charlotte Mendelson, Clementine Mendelson, Elaine O'Dwyer, Kate Saunders, Louisa Saunders, Joseph Schwartz, Richard Skinner, Gillian Stern and Alison Wilkinson; and especially to Jonny Geller, Selina Walker and all at Curtis Brown and Arrow.

NOW

I have seen Pollard again. I'm sure I have; or was it an illusion?

I am certain it was Pollard's face, on a man slowly turning his head in a cul-de-sac six streets away. That face many years on, ballooned and pouched as an ageing radish, but with the blue-grey eyes that gazed at our childhoods. How can a face be recognised in a moment after the passing of so many decades?

I have never stopped thinking about all that Crowsley Beck brought on us, all that my sweet mother went through after we had moved there. Arthur Pollard was a big part of that. I have been looking for him all this time, even while I was scared he would find me. I think it was Pollard. I vomited shortly after I arrived home.

THEN

1963

I

The village green of Crowsley Beck: you never did
see such a sparkling run of grass. Only the flagpole
socket where the children laid traps of twigs
for strolling adults interrupted the green with a
slot of air.

There they were, village children marching together,
boys with shorts and shining hair, girls in kilts, plaits
and pleats, crossing the grass past the ducks towards
the war memorial, the elm leaves laughing light. The
brother and sister from the big house at the end of
the village; the boys from next to the post office; and
four of the Crale children.

The Crale children: Rosemary and Jennifer Crale
the twins, the boy Bob, and baby Caroline. They
walked over the green on this their first Sunday in

the village, bright bright against the grass. The twins: ruddy Rosemary with her hair band and red cable knit; Jennifer the angel face with her yellow plaits, her blue eyes in a bed of lashes; and their little brother in his shirt and Sunday tie. The baby slept in her perambulator like a good girl. A low-flying plane darkened the green, birds chorused, and this was surely the prettiest village in all of England. It was so exactly how a village should be that crews from the studios at Elstree came to film there.

The other Crale child straggled behind. This was Evangeline, who was dressed as a Victorian and had rain for hair. She loitered, then dipped into the river, her lacy petticoats muddied, her pinafore greyed; she guttered in the others' shining, blanked out by their shadows. Where the other Crales were clean with health and Jennifer was doll-beautiful, Evangeline was a grubby, transparent girl, dragging her feet and slipping away. Her face was scrawny, with eyes set too far apart. On her head bristled a dirty nylon ribbon of daisies.

The checked frocks and short skirts stamped across the green, pushing the baby, ignoring Evangeline, and sometimes she was hardly there, though villagers stared and stared at her that first weekend. Then she appeared among the swans, drab and pale in the gnat-shade. She seemed to be talking to someone, but it was uncertain who.

'Well, hello,' said Gregory Dangerfield to the children's mother, Rowena Crale, who stood outside her new house, number 3 The Farings, looking up at the roof with her hand on her brow like a visor, as she had seen models do.

Her legs were on display as she stood balanced in high heels on the rubble while her builder weighed into the walls, despite the objections of the South Herts Historical Association and the Crowsley Beck Preservation Society.

She turned, slowly, the glare making the man prickle in front of her eyes. She was nervous about meeting the villagers, wondering whether she looked too urban, too smart.

'Hello?' she said with slight enquiry. She had a neatly cut profile, her hair twisted into a high bun.

'Gregory Dangerfield,' he said, extending his hand. He was dressed in a suit for church, but his tie was loose in the heat. 'I live over there.'

'Pleased to meet you,' she said, taking his hand after a moment's hesitation, then blushing.

'And you're knocking the two houses together?'

'Oh. Yes. Growing family.' She smiled, appeasingly, and glanced up at the house, its many-paned windows framed by pleasant arches, its faded red brick faintly undulating with age.

The builder, who was behind schedule and working at the weekends, carried a hod out of the front door, and Gregory nodded at him. 'Terrible noise,' he said.

'Apologies, Mr Dangerfield,' said the builder.

'No, no, I'm not complaining. Something doesn't want to give in there.'

The builder said nothing, sweat beading over his face.

'It doesn't,' he said.

'Can I take a look?' said Gregory, peering into the gloom through the open door that made the dust-swirling cottage appear like a carcass, steaming in the sun.

'Oh. Yes,' said Rowena, and she pressed her hands, which felt damp, to her skirt.

'My word, this must be a stubborn blighter,' said Gregory, tipping his head in the direction of the builder. 'I've heard you working on it all week.'

'You's telling me,' said the builder, and in the shade, his sweat rose. A hole was knocked into the plaster and brick of the wall between the two cottages, with another attempt abandoned higher up. 'It doesn't want to come.'

'Let me have a go,' said Gregory Dangerfield, and

he folded his jacket on a chair, rolled up his shirt-sleeves, and swung a mallet at the plaster. The wall protested, groaning like a heifer. 'I've barely made a mark!' he said. 'Come on, man. Put some back into it.'

He picked up a chisel, swung his arms, muscles honed on two dozen summers of gully fielding, and sank the chisel into the dividing wall. It screamed, and a chunk of plaster fell off.

A new smell met the sweat, like cat urine, or tomcat spray, seeping from stains.

'Good Lord,' said Gregory. There was a settling groaning of plaster. More damp oozed, a metallic smell overlaying the cat odour.

'It can't be done,' said the builder, shaking his head.

'I've never heard you say such a thing, Pollard,' said Gregory, and took another swing. 'Of course it can.'

The mallet bounced with a ring off the wall, which groaned in a higher pitch. Clumps of horsehair and strands of longer tail or mane clung to rusty stains, a glimpse of brick.

'Gosh,' said Rowena, standing a few feet back in the shade and feeling faint suddenly. 'That wall is bulging now.'

It seemed to have become subtly swollen and shiny, as though pregnant. Like her own stomach, she thought, which had still not settled to its former shape after yet another baby. It was a trick of the light. It receded.

'No, Mrs Crale. It's not shifting,' said Pollard the builder.

'It's an illusion caused by the heat,' said Gregory, turning to her, and she caught his gaze. His dark brown eyes seemed to wander momentarily over her body. His hair, of the same brown, was clean-cut, soldier-short at the neck, yet there was something boyish, almost playful, to its slight spring over his brow. 'And you've moved in already?'

'We've had to,' said Rowena, her voice a little unsteady. 'In here and into the other cottage. It's round the corner. It'll be an L-shaped house I suppose, eventually. Is that what's making this so difficult? The corner?'

'No,' said Pollard.

'Let me have a look,' said Gregory at the same time.

He walked out of the front door that gave on to the lane beside the green and let himself in through the gate to number 2 The Farings, where a series of lodgers had lived until recently, and turned to the walls and roof. A tiny path led through a choke of shrubbery to a glimpse of a small vegetable garden and fields beyond. Behind the shrubbery, running the length of the cottages and their gardens, was his own property, the lawn leading to what was known locally as 'the Big House'.

The builder went to his tool bag, and Rowena stood alone. The dusty air seemed unsettled in the contrast between glare and shade, and she instinctively wanted the men to come back, or to go outside herself. There was an impression she couldn't pin down, that the house was already inhabited. Moving in there didn't feel like a fresh beginning; but she knew the house was overlaid with memories of all the years her mother-in-law had lived there.

'The cottages are similar but not identical – they may have been built at different times. It may have been an external wall originally,' said Gregory, with a vague show of authority that Rowena sensed was designed to calm a flustered woman. 'Pollard will get through it.'

'I do hope so. We're all squashed in. I'm not sure it's going to be – very big even when this is finished. My husband imagined this would have all been completed a fortnight ago.'

'The old woman who lived on this side—'

'My mother-in-law,' murmured Rowena.

'Ah. Makes sense now. And I'm glad to be rid of those lodgers on the other side. Did your mother-in-law keep pets?'

'Not for a long time.'

The damp in the wall seemed to be spreading now it was released. Gregory pressed his finger to it, smelled it. 'Cat,' he said. 'Distinctively.'

'But how?'

'Who knows? A herd of kittens nesting in some boarded-up fireplace there? There's certainly a stable's worth of horsehair. Your wall perhaps doubles as a livestock pen. Mrs . . . ?'

'Oh, I'm sorry. Crale. Rowena Crale. My husband is Douglas. He will be here after church.'

Two of Pollard's men had arrived for a renewed battering at the wall.

'It almost seems almost as though it were *rotting*,' said Rowena. 'It needs to come down.'

Builders' grunts followed, and the crash of three hammers chipped a piece of brick. The wall groaned, resisted, shuddered.

'Dynamite,' said Gregory, accompanying Rowena out into the sunshine. 'Why did you use Arthur Pollard, by the way?'

'Oh, my husband found him. Through a recommendation, I think. It was harder, from London. You know him. His work?'

'I'm sure he's fine. He lives in the village, but people round here tend to use other builders. Most of his employment is in Radlett, and even as far as St Albans, I understand.'

'Oh. Oh dear.'

'No, I'm sure his work's fine. Villagers are lemmings. As you'll see. Several of them do use Mrs Pollard's kindergarten, though. You've been living in London?'

'Yes.' She nodded, in an abstracted fashion.

'Welcome to Crowsley Beck. Twenty miles from Piccadilly Circus, but a different world entirely. There, look, the bells are drowning out old Pollard. You and your husband must come round for drinks.'

The bells paused. The wall screamed, protested, cried.

'You'll have an interesting-shaped room there,' said Gregory, and Rowena nodded, a line of anxiety on her forehead smoothed by her smile.

It was only after he had left and the dust had settled that she smelled another smell, barely there over the affronting odours. She turned, and her nose caught the faintest drift of women's perfume. She recognised it, but she couldn't think what it was.

The children wheeled, breathless, into church as the bells bowled over the green, the vicar almost bowing in his greeting as this large new family swelled his congregation, and Evangeline slipped off among the reeds.

The hymns sounded through the village.

There across the green from the church was the post office and shop with its large Wall's freezer, then the duck pond, the war memorial, the pub, the copse; on the other side of the post office, the winding back lanes with their cottages. Pansies grew in baskets and the rooks cawed black across the green. The whistling roads of south Hertfordshire led outside the village past flat ploughed fields of crow and flint, bone-shaped knobbles of pudding-stone among the crops, to the stables where village children rode. Then to the private schools, boys' and girls', and then to the aerodrome where the men flew on Saturdays, and beyond that, the nuclear power station with its spherical reactor partly concealed in a dip. The school for retarded, handi-capped or unmanageable children was in the other direction: Evangeline Crale's new school from September.

Pollard and his men carried on working while the Crales were at church. With no one to watch it, the wall began to spew its guts, hair and lime putty with foul brown dust and eructations of damp. It moaned like a tree falling.

'Where is Eva?' said Rowena, scanning the green after church. In her heart, she always feared that one day Evangeline, who roamed, might simply fail to return. The country, she thought, with a new realisation, would afford her more opportunities to wander. 'Where *is* Eva?'

Evangeline, known as Eva to her family, was hiding in the stream. Its flow had fallen to a trickle, but its banks were still putty cool, and she lay her head against them and found their mosses as her pillow. The sky above was a brilliant blue through leaves. Her invisible friend Freddie had arrived just after her in the village, and she hugged him in the stream, for he was younger than her, and she chatted reassuringly to him. She sidled near the new house before the others had crossed the green from church, and Pollard saw her, and smiled. Other villagers loitered at gates for gossip after church, and stared and whispered in consternation or amusement. They had never seen a girl like this. Was she in fancy dress? Was she something from one of the film companies? But there were inconsistencies: her hair ribbon was synthetic, her mud-streaked petticoats revealed sandals.

Rowena crossed the green, becoming too hot inside her blouse and worrying about the lamb that was roasting in the old gas oven. There was a splash of light on a window in the roof of her new house that made her look up, then close her eyes against its glare. She felt conspicuous: she was watched. She didn't know how to behave, somehow, within a small village, and she felt awkwardly certain that she was incongruous, and that Evangeline would be bringing shame to the family already. Three of her children walked in a neat line beside her, while she pushed the youngest in the pram that had seen her through five babies, even the twins lying head to toe.

Evangeline was kneeling near the fence of number 3 and picking daisies from the verge. Her hair and hands were brown with mud. Her small sharp teeth were showing in her feral face as she sang a nursery rhyme to herself. She looked up and glanced at the others, then looked back down. 'I will get my revenge,' she muttered to Freddie, whom no one else could see.

'Evangeline, go inside. How dare you, really how dare you? There isn't sufficient hot water for so very much washing,' said Rowena, tutting at her third daughter with an impatience that met terrible sympathy, and Evangeline merely hung her head before going up to the bathroom under the eaves, where the ceiling sloped sharply and only the loofah was unpacked. In the bath, which she ran cold on the hot day, she skimmed her hands over her body. Then she let herself cry.

Downstairs, the roasting lamb was making the kitchen explosive with heat, and the wall still screamed like a sow. Pollard and his men had taken to it again after a short break. Rowena put her hands to her ears, feeling heat and noise crowding in on her with a plunge of panic about how she would manage to cook for seven in this ancient kitchen, and told her children to go upstairs to play. Jennifer, the beauty, lingered and gazed at her mother, running her corn-fat plaits through circled thumbs and fingers, up and down, as she often did, and said, 'It's all right, Mummy. It's all all right.'

Rowena smiled at her, and the combination of Jennifer's placidity and loveliness calmed her. Looking at her was like encountering a breathtaking countryside view; it soothed the soul. Rowena had never in her life seen such a beautiful child. How had she given birth to a girl who looked like an exquisitely wrought doll? She felt proud, though she knew that nature's trickery was outside her hands. With the exception of poor Eva, the others were healthy and appealing, but not out of the ordinary. Jennifer Crale resembled a doctored photograph. She could be a young film star in *Life* magazine, with her rose-dusted cheeks, her row of pearly teeth with their endearing gap in the middle, her eyes so large and intensely blue it was almost difficult to land upon her gaze. Her lashes seemed to weigh her eyelids down, like the Victorian dolls that Eva treasured with their glaze of pink, their sooty slotted eyes and rosebud smiles.

'What a *pretty* girl,' the vicar's wife had already said.

'You insult her,' said the verger. 'The girl is quite beautiful.'

'Thank you,' said Rowena, who had heard it all before, but enjoyed it, always, anew, with the same sense of surprise and lack of entitlement. 'Thank you.'

Rowena now prodded the lamb and gagged slightly at the steam from the potatoes. She felt trapped in some stranger's scullery, the stove an unsteady monster, old fly strips hanging just beyond her reach.

'It's too hot in here,' she said to Jennifer. 'Will you go and fetch the baby's sunshade from her room?'

'Yes,' said Jennifer. She hesitated. She picked up a spoon and stood there playing with it.

'Don't you *like* doing things for your baby sister?' said Rowena. 'You didn't want to go up to fetch her from her nap earlier.'

'Oh, I *do*,' said Jennifer. 'Of course, Mummy. It's just I get a bit lost on that side of the house. I – if I go upstairs.'

'Darling! You've been there dozens of times when Granny lived there.'

'Yes,' said Jennifer, then she gave her smile with its charming dimple, and went out into the garden and round on to the lane to enter number 3's front door, the only way of accessing that side until the dividing wall was knocked down.

It was ridiculous to cook a roast on a day like this, thought Rowena. They could have had a salad with ham or eggs, followed by a jelly, but Douglas expected his Sunday roast, even when the temperature must be in the nineties and she had only an oven that wobbled on its legs, rocking with each blow to the wall. She turned at a movement in the passage outside the kitchen, but it was merely the play of sun and shadow. The carrots were turning to mush, so she went to gather her children.

The twins played in the garden with the baby, but her only son Bob was upstairs in number 3, the front cottage. She ran into that section and climbed the stairs, and felt momentarily sad at the top. She stood still. Bob was kneeling on the floor above the stubborn wall.

He grinned up at her. His rusting golliwog bucket was half full of a crumbling brown substance. He was digging into the floor itself.

'Bob!' she cried. 'Whatever are you doing?' She snatched his beach spade. 'What *are* you doing?'

'Digging floor, Mummy! Look, I make a hole.'

He spun round and kicked his heel against the hole, gouging up more rotting wood resembling earth.

'Soon on the other side!'

Rowena knelt down. 'It's revolting!' she said to him. Tentatively, she pressed her finger where he had dug. It was soft and damp. The floorboards were decaying; the thumping below shook the whole building. A mildewed scent stuck to her finger, and as she rose, she again caught the perfume. It was familiar, but she couldn't remember what it was. For the briefest flash of a moment, a face came to her, an old face crying, but it was her mind playing tricks, and she turned it off like a light switch.

'I hear dem,' said Bob conversationally. 'I keeping worms in this!' He was stirring the contents of his bucket with his spade. 'I hear dem talk at sleep time,' he said, almost chattering to himself. 'Walk.'

'What are you talking about, Bob?' said Rowena mildly, but she wasn't really concentrating; she leaned against a wall and closed her eyes as it juddered against her cheek. Where was Douglas? He had gone off to the pub for a half-pint — something he never did in London — with one of the new neighbours after church with some excuse about the village cricket team, and now he wouldn't even be back to carve the joint. She pictured him striding in with his shirtsleeves rolled up as the joint congealed, wielding the carving knife as though he were caressing a woman. She felt sick.

'Please,' she called down weakly. 'Leave the wall. Just while we have luncheon. Perhaps – perhaps you could start on the windows?'

'Yes, Mrs Crale,' called back Arthur Pollard.

Evangeline lay in her bathtub, watching bubbles cling to her thighs like little river insects, and wringing more mud out of her hair. The warmth of her tears spread pleasingly into the cold of the bathwater. She lay her head under the surface and dreamed, planning to hide potatoes from lunch in her petticoat pockets. She was happier up here, close to where her grandmother had slept, in her air, in her love. She climbed out.

Arthur Pollard suddenly appeared in the doorway.

'I apologise,' he said.

'No, it's all right,' said Evangeline, blushing, and for a moment she was pinned by indecision and stood in front of him in just her underwear.

'Was going to wash me hands. I'll be out of your way.' His fair hair was further lightened with dust.

She tossed her layers of muddied clothes into the washing basket and scampered out of the room, then went to collect a fresh gored petticoat and a chemise from her grandmother's trunk that she kept in the bedroom she shared with the baby, and slipped into the kitchen where she ate a portion of lamb that had been saved for her, hiding half a dozen cold potatoes to eat later.

Douglas Crale dozed in his chair after lunch, his shirt buttons undone, while the twins helped their mother clear up. Eva rocked the crying baby, as she was best at that and her mother bothered her less if she helped with little Caroline. A railway set had been laid out for Bob. Eva held the baby against her chest, the cotton of her frock bearing the faint yellow lines of long folding, and she chattered at her, letting her pull strands of her hair and kissing her with the edges of her teeth. Soon she had her asleep, and she slipped upstairs, leaving the others to their afternoon. Her age-faded clothes dipped into the shadows of the stairwell, and no one noticed her leave, because they were used to her disappearances and her dresses were the hue of shadowed walls and her hair the dullness of a mouse back.

At the top of the stairs sat Pollard. He smelled of the carbolic soap Rowena had put in the bathroom for his use, and he had a packet of sandwiches in wax paper on his lap.

'Want one?' he said.

Eva nodded.

She took a bite and then another. 'These are much nicer than ours,' she said in her slow, low voice. 'What are they?'

'Sandwich Spread,' he said thickly through his chewing, and handed her another one. She paused, then put it in her petticoat pocket and giggled.

'Secret supply,' he said in level tones, winking at her. He had a face like a grown-up elf's, strong but fine-featured, she thought.

She laughed, but quietly, so her mother wouldn't hear her, and then smiled at him.

'*Secret* supply,' he said, still chewing, and she laughed again.

'Pollard,' she said. 'Be careful.'

'What's she called?' he said in matter-of-fact tones.

'Who?'

'You know who.'

Eva's expression froze. She tried to think of other names, other people, but only one would come to her.

'Jennifer,' she said.

He nodded. 'You like her?'

'She's my sister,' said Evangeline. 'Of course *I* do.'

He nodded. 'I ain't ever seen anyone . . .' His eyes crinkled, and focused on the distance.

'Prettier,' she said, to help him out.

'Yes, that.'

Eva shrugged. 'I'm going now,' she said.

Pollard took no notice. 'What school you lot going to go to come new term?'

'It's called . . . It's called Rag-something Place.'

'Who? You?' he said in a tone of surprise.

'Yes.'

'Ragdell Place. You aren't touched enough to go there. Ragamuffins go there. Ones that can't speak. Hooooo-ligans.' His face and eyes were bright with amusement. 'And the other ones?'

'Mummy wants, terribly *much* wants, Jennifer and Rosemary to go to St *Bede's*,' she said. 'I don't know if they will, though. She thinks Jennifer might if she works hard enough *all* summer. Bob's going to the primary school.'

He nodded. 'Bede's's only for the brains,' he said.

'I know,' she said coldly.

'You can come and see me and my wife at my place,' Pollard said. He stood up. He was taller than she would have expected, with a slightness despite his strength. His blue-grey eyes seemed to look into distance, like a sailor's, and were deep set, among small sun wrinkles.

'OK,' said Eva, brightening.

'Come tomorrow. After I've finished my morning work here. Wife'll give you a big fat custard tart.'

Eva grinned at him.

She went back to her grandmother's trunk. *Evangeline Crale* was written on it. She, among four girls, had been named after her grandmother, and her grandmother was her beloved. Her life blood. Her real mother. The kindest old woman in the world, and her parents had thought it fair to send her away so they could take over her cottage. So *they* could steal her only home, join it to the one next door they had already bought, laying their plans long ago. It was thieving. Terrible theft.

'She is simply too old, darling,' Rowena had said when the plan was first revealed. 'She needs care now. She needs to be looked after, don't you see?'

'But not by a friend. She needs her *family*,' said Eva, almost screaming. '*Us.*'

'There's not room. She will be—'

'Not *room* in *her* own house?' shrieked Eva.

Rowena was quiet for a few seconds.

'Granny needs looking after,' she said patiently.

'Grandmamma,' snapped Evangeline.

'Yes, yes, Granny, Grandmamma. Lois has offered her a home. Lois has no children, and she's experienced with older people. She's family, almost.'

'Lois is her *goddaughter*,' said Eva, this time in a hiss. She had a level, husky voice, her emphases oddly placed. 'She runs a boarding house. She won't *look* after her. It's in Scot*land*. It's too too far away. We'll never never see her again.' And she began crying, hysterically, her mouth and nose dripping over the top of the clothes her grandmother had given her.

Eva now plunged her face in the depths of the trunk in her search for her grandmother's youth, lifting just the corner of the bottom layers, which she would never take out, because then she would lose the smell of her beloved grandmother, squander it to the air, trample on her as her family had. The top layers were her clothes, her daily wear, but there were tightly folded items at the bottom she would never never sully.

2

Pollard the builder was peering round the bend on the narrow staircase that led into the sitting room of number 2. Bob was making chugging noises with his cheeks puffed out as he pushed his toy train around its tracks, and there was Jennifer bending over him building a bridge. Even in the sun-deprived room of that stunted cottage shaded by ilexes, the blue of her eyes was steel-bright against her lashes and her curved dark brows. A dimple hovered on one cheek when she smiled; the gap in her teeth seemed to channel the beam of her delight, her features almost discomfitingly perfectly arranged. That small straight bridge of a nose, lightly freckle-strewn. The calmness of the rosebud mouth when closed. The complete tranquillity of her being that broke into bubbles of delight.

'What are you doing, *Mr* Pollard?' said Eva.

'Watching 'em play,' he said.

'Yes.'

'But it's you I've invited to my house tomorrow.'

'Yes, Pollard. Can I invite Freddie? He's my friend.'

Pollard nodded in assent.

'You can't see him. *Apparently* he's imaginary.'

'That's as may be. Come in my lunch break for that big fat pie the missus is going to make you, and I can toddle back over for half an hour as well. Brinden, the house is called. Out across fields behind the stream. Or you can go round Beeck Lane and through the spinney, top of the village.'

She nodded. 'I know my way round already.'

Rowena stood in the kitchen when the dishes were cleared and sipped a sherry. A small figure flitted past the door and she looked up, expecting to see Bobby, but it was nothing, and she realised that the alcohol went to her head too quickly in the heat. Through the ilex, the rhododendron and laurel, she could catch a pale grey glimpse of the Big House, as she had heard it called.

Douglas's snuffles and sleepy starts sounded from the sitting room to a backdrop of canary chatter, and the baby had begun to cry from the path outside. Looking vaguely round for Evangeline, Rowena ignored the clamour, just for a quarter of an hour more, mentally blocking it out. She could barely believe that this house was hers, with all its low-ceilinged prettiness, its curving plaster, its nooks and cupboards and little passages. It was as though she would now be a proper woman, a grown-up wife and mistress of a lovely house at last, and not the play-acting imposter she sometimes felt herself to be. Numbers 2 and 3 The Farings were postcard cottages, age-softened and settled, with their deep-set windows and boxes of geraniums, their uneven floors and cool pantries, their small gardens tangles of mature flowers and shrubbery. The modern house in London had contained no soul, and little opportunity for her decorating dreams; The Farings, by contrast, possessed so much character, she found it hard to believe there weren't other people there. That was why she was faintly nervy, she realised, imagining movement in other rooms, because it simply didn't seem as though it was theirs yet.

She stood up straight and looked out at the garden. She was still sore from Caroline's birth; she bled all these weeks later, and she was using ingenuity to avoid Douglas, who was clearly becoming restless. She must, must lose the pregnancy weight by the end of the summer to be as trim as she had been previously despite all those babies. ('Body of a maiden,' her mother-in-law had commented after Bob's birth. It was Caroline who had tipped her.) She crept into the sitting room to avoid the grizzling, and braced herself for what she might see.

Pollard had left, finally, but the wall still seemed hunched like some wounded animal that was catching its breath. On the side where the old Mrs Crale had lived, it was covered in wallpaper, and the stains over there showed more clearly than on the paint and plaster of this side, where yellow maps with furring brown borders spread over the corner between wall and ceiling. The craters that Pollard and his men had made showed live white patches of spores or mildew clinging to brick. Horsehair hung in patches over the wallpaper with its twining trellis and bird design, birds' heads and tails cut off, as though shot, where the builders had gone through to the brick. Others were caught mid-flight by hammer blows, their poor wings blasted, cuffs and ruffs of broken paper round their necks.

Rowena held her breath. The smell: was it cat? Rat? Worse? Animal urine seemed to merge with mould. The children had all complained. Douglas had sworn he would work Pollard harder. Rowena, in her hormonal state, her breasts still full of milk, gagged. She was feeding this one herself, as she never

CALGARY
PUBLIC
LIBRARY

W R Casteil Central Library
Self Checkout
July,12,2016 14:16

39065141528842   8/2/2016
Touched

Total   1 item(s)

You have 0 item(s) ready for pickup

had the others, and she felt like a nauseated cow. Even cigarettes tasted off.

More disturbingly, as she breathed through her mouth, there was a drift of perfume over the mould, that same taste of women's scent settling on her tongue. It nagged at her. She almost knew what it was. The crying wrinkled features flashed at her. A whiff of rot or animal hit her in the back of the throat and she forgot about it, rushing to the kitchen for water.

She had such plans for this house, she thought, as she steadied herself at the sink. She had spent weeks and weeks in London, first pregnant, then cow-feeding the baby, looking at *Homemaker* and *Modern Woman* and books from the library containing designs she could never previously have afforded but just might be able to copy with the move out of London. It had felt like an obsession. Except for the wall between the cottages, number 2 was in a reasonable state to do up, but she wondered whether number 3 was rotting. It gave her a pang of worry that she dismissed by fetching elderflower cordial for the family.

Fronting the green, right in the centre of the small village, stood the most desirable cottages, number 3 The Farings at the end of a small row. Evangeline slipped from the cottage across the lane and on to the grass, and neighbours watched her. She had a small-chinned face that widened at the cheeks and brow like a blunt cat's, and eyes in which hazel muddied grey, their distance lending her a dreaming, abstracted look. Front doors were left open in the heat; men leaned against fences and smoked pipes; women rocked babies in gardens. Some of them stared openly at the sepia flickering of this strange girl in the glare; a few made disparaging comments; the wife of the milkman crossed herself.

'Freddie, Freddie,' Eva murmured, looking down, as though to a small child.

'She's talking to *herself*. How does her mother allow that child to look such a sight?' said Lana Dangerfield, descending from her husband Gregory's MGB, the magnificent little sports car that had been his present to himself when he had been made manager of the power station.

Gregory barked with laughter. 'Good for her,' he said, and he glanced at the windows of number 3 The Farings, but there were only dark small panes, the house seeming silent and sunken. Rowena Crale was absent, but voices wound down the path from number 2.

Lana Dangerfield stiffened. 'I don't find it amusing,' she said. 'The girl looks half crazed.'

'Perhaps she is.'

Lana paused. 'Ah,' she said. 'Possibly then they moved here for Ragdell Place.'

'The hellhole for halfwits?'

Lana frowned, as she so often did at her husband. 'The school for – troubled children,' she said.

'Who knows?' said Gregory idly, and stood lighting a cigarette at his own gate. The Dangerfield children, Peter and Jane, had returned from a friend's house, and Lana neatened their hair in turn as they passed through the gate.

'I'll just smoke this,' said Gregory, and he wandered across the lawn. He made his way down to the shade of the rhododendrons, the ilexes and variegated laurel at the bottom of the garden, and smoked in their shade. Number I The Farings, at the end of the path, housed only a taciturn old widower who hid himself either there or in his allotment, but number 2 was now fuller and noisier.

'Shut up,' he muttered at the crying baby, and stood there a while, but her mother didn't appear.

Evangeline paddled in the stream again, winding her way down it towards the pond, where ducks nodded. 'Come, Freddie,' she called. She glanced up at the house, checking it, and was satisfied. Afternoon softened, Rowena hushed the baby, and the actress who lived by the centre of the green walked past in her short pink floral dress, much commented on by Crowsley Beck residents. She nodded at Rowena, whose auburn chignon and profile of a model posing as an air hostess made her noticeably smart and attractive for a villager.

The twins sat down for their extra studies, the television and canary cage covered with cloths until the early evening, and Bob made the baby mud pies. 'Near *your* room. Near *my* room,' he sang to her and gave her a rough kiss so she grizzled, then he repeated it.

Rowena glimpsed the damp wall again, and this time she let out a low moan, for it seemed to be weeping. It might never succumb, she thought, and then what would they do? She had a momentary vision of a dark tunnel of recalcitrance, unspecified trouble. There was something indefinably resistant about the builder who worked on it, too. He was set on his course; he was self-contained. The other smell was now more apparent, borne by the wafts of damp. *Je Reviens*, it was called. Of course. Rowena was pleased with herself for remembering, but something about it made her uncomfortable, and she couldn't think what it was.

3

'Good morning,' said the vicar, faint bemusement crossing his face as a scrawny girl in a lightly stained Victorian child's costume walked past the post office towards Beeck Lane. He summoned his genial smile. He had a range of smiles, beams and expressions of gravity at his disposal, suitable to the occasion and the day of the week. 'Can I help you?' he said eventually.

'No, thank you,' said Evangeline in her husky voice.

He paused. 'And you are?'

'Evangeline Crale.'

'Crale . . .' said the vicar, pausing again. 'There is a new family in the village named Crale. They came to the church. You're a relation?'

'Yes,' she said. 'I *am*.'

'I hope you approve of their choice of new home,' he said, spreading a plump hand towards the green with the air of one who owned it. 'Can I help direct you? Where are you going? The family live at the other end.'

'To Poll— Mr Pollard's house.'

'I hope Mrs Pollard is there too,' said the vicar, dropping his affable tone as easily as he had adopted it.

'She is. He told me.'

Eva slipped away down a little path hung with flower baskets between cottages, her skirts sepia toned as though gas-lit under a dull sky; he waited, but she didn't reappear, and a few minutes later she was bounding across the fields, the pallor of her clothes glowing beneath clouds.

Pollard's house was bigger than it first appeared to be. An old farmhouse patchily clad in weathered rendering, it crouched in a dip of field on the edge of the village. Up close, there seemed to be no end to it: a low extension at a right angle behind the main front, outbuildings both intact and in various states of collapse; a disordered alley of greenhouse, sheds, empty animal pens. Fertiliser bags and rusting sheets of corrugated iron seemed to cover mounds of earth or vegetation, with chickens wandering loose and rabbits in a makeshift cage. It was clearly no longer a working farm. Cats seemed to be everywhere. There were several noticeably large cats among them. Eva was unsure whether to enter through a door under a sagging porch, where the windows were blank, or a side door near a caravan and vegetable patch. She chose the side door. A vast tortoiseshell wound itself round her skirts as she stood waiting, and she jumped as she glimpsed its size, absorbing it as some lynx, some escaped creature from a circus or zoo. But it was just a domestic cat, its broad brindled face wrinkling in supplication as it looked up to her with an insistent mew, and she stroked it, its tail filling her hand. Her other hand was tugged by Freddie.

A woman stood at the door in a housecoat.

'Come in, dear,' she said in a gentle voice. She did not, as most people did, hesitate or stare at Evangeline's clothes. 'I was expecting you.'

'Oh. Oh. Yes. Hello, *Mrs* Pollard. I'm—'

'Evangeline is the prettiest name I ever heard,' she said. 'I have been thinking about it ever since Arthur said it, my dear.' Her voice was soft, measured, a notch more refined than her husband's.

'My daddy really wanted a boy by the time I was born, and I wasn't, so then he de*manded* I was at least called after his mother. And I'm so *glad.*'

'Yes, lovely. I've been wanting to know. What are your brothers' and sisters' names, dear? I'm expecting they're pretty and fancy too.'

'Rosemary, Jennifer, Bob and Caroline,' she said.

'Oh,' said Mrs Pollard. She hesitated, her plump face unmoving. Her eyes were childlike in their pale blue roundness, and she wore her hair unfashionably, in a sort of chopped bob with a thick fringe that lent further unsettling aspects of youth to her appearance. 'Well, you have the prettiest of all, then.'

'They call me Eva mostly.'

'I shall always call you Evangeline. Come in, come in and have your lunch I made especially for you. Don't trip over the cats, my dear. Pretty clothes. Where did you get them?'

'From my grandmother,' said Eva tightly. '*Her* name is Evangeline—'

A whistling sounded from behind the caravan, and Pollard himself turned up, covered in dust.

'Hello, dear,' said Mrs Pollard.

'I'm famished. They should never be knocking that wall down,' he said to Eva. 'It doesn't want to go. It's clinging on. Given me a giant of a blister.'

'They should never knock into my *grandmother's* house,' she said.

'It's a stubborn one, I'll say that for it. Let me demonstrate you my sheds first,' said Pollard, handing his jacket to his wife, then he showed Eva the coal shed where many cats lived, and she gazed at their distended abdomens, their club-like heads. 'Some of them is with kitten,' he said. He led her past a tangle of chicken wire over some old planks and showed her his greenhouses, and the potting shed that contained the tools and materials for his hobby: he made flowers, primarily roses, from moulded plastic while the wireless played, and the best of them he gave to his wife. He had his own little stove in there, congealed with grease, a kettle and a toaster, and he painted portraits and landscapes in oil. Outside, bramble reared over collapsed cow sheds, discarded twine tangling with thistle and teasel.

'There's so much. Anything could be hidden here,' said Eva.

A slight drizzle was cooling the air, drawing snails on to the dock leaves as they walked back to the house. 'You can help me with my roses,' said Pollard. 'You're a clever girl, I think.'

Mrs Pollard had laid out a lunch of cold roast beef, beetroot salad, and a bed of a custard tart, half of which she could take home. Bunches of the roses were arranged in vases in the dining room, which contained a thick persistent smell of milk that settled at the back of Eva's throat.

They were so kind to her, a little tear started to

creep from the corner of her eye, and she brushed it away, for she feared that if she began to cry, she would never stop. Adults customarily shrank from her, ignored her, or addressed her like a simpleton. At her primary school, they had tied her to her chair to keep her in lessons, then tied her to another at lunch; but largely, she was allowed to disappear, and if people didn't want her, such absences were her preference.

Mrs Pollard had closed the dining-room windows against the drizzle, but she opened them again, and Eva was aware of a noise drifting into the room from outside. Children. Babies.

'May I be excused?' she said, and she wandered to the window. She gasped.

'Let's go and see them, dear,' said Mrs Pollard. Her voice was so soft, it was as though it had been sweetened.

On the sloping lawn with its untidy rockery that backed on to fields, then the elms and horse chestnuts that sheltered the centre of the village, sat pram after pram; played child after child.

'My little nursery, my dear,' said Mrs Pollard in tones that were so soothing, Eva shivered. 'I look after some of the village children for a few hours. It's almost bottle time.'

As though by rote, a mass grizzling set up. Eva

skipped over the lawn, and, reaching through a cat net, she plucked a bawling infant from its perambulator and rocked it. As it quietened, she lifted its neighbour with her other arm and held it to her chest, comforting the two babies at once until they ceased crying. The others were silent only once their mouths were plugged with rubber teats, and they drained their bottles, their rhythmic gulping like so many calves.

Groups of cats gathered round in a cacophony of competitive mewling, and Mrs Pollard fed them in bowls from the same vast vat of milk she had made up for the babies.

'Bring your sister if you want next time,' said Pollard, setting off back to the village after lunch. He was upright, oddly graceful in his strength.

Eva's face darkened into its usual pinched little heart. Pollard's words hit her like a blow to her middle.

'I thought—' she almost sobbed, but she couldn't finish. 'That is *what they always*—'

'I like you the best!' he said cheerfully.

She suppressed a gasp. 'Do you—'

'You know I do. Come September, you can help with the babies and the roses if you want to escape the mad school.'

'You know I *am* not mad, don't you?'

'Course you aren't. Nothing wrong with you.'

'Yes. Thank you. I'd like to help with the children.'

'There's many!'

'Do you have some too?'

'No,' he said quite brightly. 'None born to us. Don't suppose there will be now. So the missus, she collects cats and children. She doesn't collect them, exactly – they come to her.'

By early afternoon, Rowena had cleared away lunch, and was increasingly anxious because the Crowsley, Beershott and Leas Wives' Association was coming over to The Farings for drinks that evening, and though she had warned them of the building works, a damp oozing wall would be an embarrassment she could barely contemplate. She took a sip of sherry. The twins were playing outside, and Bob and baby Caroline were napping. A door shut upstairs, and she stood up at the sound, pausing, but then she remembered how crooked Pollard had said the top floor was. She tried to read the newspaper. It seemed she never used her mind these days, barely stretching it since she had been at grammar school – those precious few years when she soared now contained like a dream – and she tried to concentrate on Premier Khrushchev's nuclear test ban treaty. Pollard harried his men and took up his tools again with renewed vigour, while Eva, who had been out all day, sloped off once more. 'I am taking Freddie out to air,' she muttered as she left.

'Eva!' Rowena called, but she had gone.

There was someone in the area leading to the downstairs lavatory. Who was it? Rowena ran through the five children and their whereabouts. No. There was no one. She felt confused as though waking from sleep. Bob was in his bedroom and Caroline was sleeping in her pram. So why was there the feeling of another child in the house? Near the doorway. Freddie? She tutted, annoyed – Evangeline's disturbances were infecting her brain.

She walked into the room next door where Pollard was working after his lunch break. A battery of hammer blows hit the house, and the wall seemed to bow, tense, suffer in small explosions of plaster and wallpaper.

'This isn't right,' murmured Rowena, and again she wondered if she could smell the *Je Reviens*.

Pollard heard her. 'It's safe, Mrs Crale. We're using an I-Beam.'

Bob came down from his after-lunch nap.

'Have you slept, my darling?' Rowena almost sang, attempting to sound cheerful. She scooped him up and kissed him. She drew in his smell. It was the best perfume in the world: hot cheek.

Bob shook his head, grinning at his mother. 'They up there,' he said.

'Who was up there, darling?'

'Dem. Noises. Peoples.'

'There's no one up there, darling. The building work must have disturbed you.'

Bob shrugged, and swung his head from side to side like a pendulum, making silly faces until Rowena laughed and kissed him again.

'Out of the house now,' she said, taking his hand, and led him to the sandpit where baby Caroline lay in her pram, her eyes reflecting clouds. The twins were on the green. Eva was where Eva was. No one ever knew where, but she looked after herself, and she came back.

The wall let out a bellowing groan and dust belched through the open window. Rowena patted Bob and ran inside. Damp clung; hair bristled in the plaster. Pollard had all three of his men there with some extra casual labourers, and issuing a warning to Rowena, they all took to the wall at once. It screamed like wood splitting, and a large section caved in. Inexplicably, Rowena felt tears in her eyes. She had a momentary sense that it was quite hopeless, that this was all wrong, that it would never be right. She tried to steady her breathing. The labourers carried on, battering like crazed men, and the wall spewed a surge of wetness, stinking of cats. She called her husband in London to tell him that it was becoming unbearable, tensing her hands as he talked impatiently of employing explosives, engineers, decent builders. The hammers began a fresh round.

'My word. This is fascinating.' Gregory Dangerfield stood in the doorway.

He had come home from the power station for a late lunch; his dog, which had a few lumps under the skin that seemed to be proliferating, lay slumped on the path outside.

Rowena turned to him, his wide-shouldered figure outlined against the sun, his shirtsleeves rolled up as ever.

'Hello,' she said, intensely grateful for the presence of a man who could take charge.

'This is the most stubborn section of masonry I've yet had the pleasure of encountering,' he said, lighting a cigarette. He nodded at Pollard.

'I barely know what to do,' said Rowena, hurting her palms.

'Let me lend you my hammer drill,' he said, laying his hand momentarily on her shoulder.

Pollard put down his tools.

'It belongs to the power station,' said Gregory. 'It will blast through it.'

He issued some brief instructions to Pollard and scrawled him a note.

'It has to be finished. I have the Wives' Association here tonight,' said Rowena, then her mouth twitched with self-consciousness, almost amusement, as she heard herself.

'Oh, those hens,' said Gregory. 'I don't mean my wife, of course.' He glanced over his shoulder at Pollard, and slowly drank the gin Rowena offered him, talking to her, then a second.

'You're the most beautiful thing I've ever seen,' he said, his voice low and steady.

Rowena's cheeks flared crimson. She played the words back, to be sure he had said them.

'I—' she said. 'I'd better think about dinner. Douglas will be home before long.'

Pollard appeared with a large electric hammer drill, and he and his men turned on the wall. They attacked it like a firing squad, and all that could be heard was the deafening battery of blows. A stench of cat and putrid damp ballooned through the air and Rowena and Gregory went outside, where baby Caroline was crying. A few houses away, Lesley Gore was singing loudly on someone's wireless. They heard a scream like a death cry, a caged bear making one last attempt to escape before slaughter, then the sobs and oozings of gas.

Rowena ran back inside. The two cottages were joined, a gaping expanse of air between. Moisture spread over the floor. *Je Reviens* again. There seemed to be sections of mane in the leftover plaster, layers even of a parchmenty substance that resembled dry skin among the rusty stains. There was hair that looked like no horse's. It was slightly curled.

'Is that a pig's tail or something?' said Rowena, unsteady on her feet, and Gregory snatched it from the plaster where it nestled. Frowning in distaste, he tossed it through the open window into the shrubbery.

'What *was* it?' she asked.

He shook his head and shrugged, not looking at her.

Eva appeared. The wall was down, dead, and it looked like a pelt. Men were standing around, sweating, exhausted after the kill. Pollard was trembling with exertion; there was dust and hair all over the floor, shattered brick, an uneasy quietness in the house. None of them, Eva could see, was quite comfortable. The canary was silent. She lifted up the cloth. It had died.

She began to shake as a fresh surge of anger hit her.

'Mummy!' she shouted, in a strangled staccato, so different from her usual low rumble.

'Hello, my chickabiddy,' said Pollard, out of Rowena's earshot.

'How *dare you, dare you*, this is, *this* is—' said Eva to her mother, but she couldn't finish. They had killed the canary; they had killed the wall. They had stolen the house, and now it was dying in front of them.

'Darling, not now,' said Rowena, laying her hand on Eva's shoulder, as Gregory had done to her, and noticing that she was tottering slightly on her heels.

Evangeline was crying against the remaining small section of wall, her face pressed to the ripped wallpaper; it had belonged to her grandmother with her dear, frail kindness, and they had not wanted her.

'You stole the house,' she hissed.

'What?' said Rowena.

'You wanted to purloin *her house.*'

Rowena frowned.

'You should *not* have destroyed her home and STOLEN IT,' shouted Eva.

Rowena put her hands over her ears.

'You must have known what it could have done to her. Mother. What was she supposed *to* do?'

Rowena jolted as though slapped, and Eva shouted

once more right in her face, then went upstairs, and cried on her bed.

Rowena trembled, angry with Eva, trying to be angrier, to fill the space where guilt was trying to get at her. She looked through the laurel at Gregory's lawn; but of course he had returned to the power station. She turned, thinking she had seen Bob pass the door, but there was no sound and the figure had, after all, seemed a little taller. She called out Bob's name, but he wasn't there. She was momentarily puzzled. She was still shaking from Eva's outburst, but Gregory's words laid a warm trail through her. Her breast leaked milk, and she stabbed at it impatiently with a tissue.

'*You're the most beautiful thing I've ever seen,*' she remembered.

No, Jennifer is the most beautiful, she thought as the twins returned. She had the sweetest demeanour. Rowena had so many children, she could acknowledge the beautiful, and the not beautiful, she thought. Her husband would have preferred more sons, she knew with a twinge of misgiving, but at least, after a big gap following the shock of Evangeline – strange wistful face with its wide-apart eyes and uneven gaze forming in toddlerhood; temper tantrums from birth – she had given him their boy.

Being a third girl must be difficult, she thought now, with a sudden stab of sympathy for poor Eva, Douglas's wish for a sturdy red-cheeked son to call his own all too apparent. His insistence that the third girl be named after his mother was patently an obstinate act of self-compensation that Rowena argued against with no success. And the two Evangelines had loved each other from the start. From the time she could speak, Eva would beg to visit her grandmother in Crowsley Beck, the journey from north London a short one, and old Evangeline Crale had nurtured, cosseted, adored her granddaughter as no one else had, dismissing her strangeness, giving her her own clothes, dolls, gewgaws, possessions that made the twins screw up their noses or sneeze.

Douglas had no patience with Eva's behaviour; Rowena herself was torn between impatience and sorrow. Increasingly, Eva was absent, and that, in truth, suited them all.

4

Ragdell Place was along one of those fast straight roads, past a nurses' training college, on the way to Radlett. Evangeline wanted to laugh when, a few days later, she went for her introductory morning at the school for backward children, for Mongols and idiots. She looked askance at the expensive colour photos on the corridor walls. A few cripples seemed to be thrown into the mix, callipers beside blank stares. She smiled to herself, and resolved to perform, to keep them all happy. Ragdell Place featured many strange chairs and locks, and she could ascertain already how to get out of the buildings and the grounds.

'I cannot get my child out of these – these clothes,' Rowena said, sweeping her hand towards Evangeline, but unable to look at her. Eva had dressed herself in her finest, her grandmother's church best, with her most intricately embroidered petticoats. She had brought a hoop with her, but Rowena had made her rest it against the gates, and she tugged off Eva's bonnet as they approached the school. Freddie, too, was in full attendance, Eva addressing him in the back of the car in elaborate prolonged monologues until Rowena had shouted at her to stop. She was irritated beyond measure by her daughter's ubiquitous imaginary friend. Eva decided to give them exactly what they wanted or expected, for she had become expert at that, and she was taciturn, she muttered to Freddie, who had run up a tree, and occasionally she gurned.

The child truly looks like a feral cat in a gown, thought Rowena, slightly frightened. She tried to show affection to compensate for the thought, but Evangeline turned to her with her row of sharp little teeth and dishwater hair and fell into a cloud of melancholy on the way home, and she simply did not know what to do with her.

'Help me, God,' she muttered. Eva needed punishing, she thought, but she somehow evaded discipline, and Rowena only occasionally had the heart to mete it out. She had spanked her that very morning in an attempt to make her wear normal clothes, after many previous failed attempts, and it had felt like abusing a wraith. Douglas had less tolerance for her behaviour, but no more success.

As Rowena swung into the village in her turquoise Anglia, Evangeline stared at the children Peter and Jane in their oversized estate car, being driven the other way by their mother Mrs Dangerfield. The Dangerfield dog, a collie, was in the luggage space. Pollard had told her that it ran around the fields all day by the power station and came home dazed. The children stared back at Evangeline, but she stared harder at the boring boy and girl who had a field of a garden to run through, two tortoises, two gardeners, and a mother who did nothing. She out-stared them, showed them her teeth a little, and laughed.

The village's resident actress, source of local excitement and disapproval, was, on this sunny day, wearing a peaked cap with a swirly lime-coloured skirt that fell above the knees. She had parked her brand new Hillman Imp, a baby blue that set off her skirt, and she was talking to the twins.

'I say,' she said to Rowena through the car window. 'When the film people come scouting, they're sure to spot your Jennifer. Remember I told you first. Toodle pip.'

Rosemary stood on the green; Evangeline got

out of the car; Jennifer looked uninterested, her eyes expressionless yet fathomless, a reed-fringed crystal pond as deep as it was empty of all but blueness. Seeing them in a line, Rowena wondered, as everyone else wondered, how such different girls could be sisters. There was a certain well-fed glow to both twins, a roundness of cheek, but Jennifer's danced into a dimple while darker Rosemary's remained stolid. Eva with her drenched tabby appearance was simply an unrelated creature, it seemed, here on the English green, by the elm trees, the pantiles.

A small Scottish man who lived at the end of the lane behind the pub was loitering on the edge of the green, watching.

'What a get-up, lassie,' he muttered to Evangeline.

'I'm sorry?' said Evangeline. She turned away from him and stuck her nose in the air.

'Like your grandmammy.'

'Yes, *hers*.'

'Heart were broken. Reet tragic.'

'I know. *I* know,' said Eva stiffly, her back still turned to him.

'Sometimes I think she hasna left at all!'

'What do you mean?' said Eva sharply, but Rowena was watching him, and he scuttled swiftly away.

*

At the house, now named simply The Farings to the consternation of the man at number 1, Pollard and his men were making good the plaster that bordered the large opening in the wall, forming a gentle arch. Apart from the stains on the ceiling, which would be removed when it was replastered, it now looked as though nothing untoward had happened. The old wall was gone, just its borders remaining, like a stiff tanned skin.

'Come over,' Pollard said in a friendly whisper to Eva. 'Saturday.'

Eva nodded slowly.

He seemed to be waiting for something.

'I shall bring my sister,' she said. She offered it like a gift, she knew; something that was in her power. Her heart jerked into a run of unsteady beats.

'All of 'em,' said Pollard surprisingly. 'The missus would like to see the baby.'

'*Yes*, Pollard,' said Eva, smiling, and went outside. The face was in the window, as she had hoped it might be.

Rowena inspected the house. The light fell in quite a different way through the larger L-shaped double room, glaring on quarry tiles and bouncing pleasingly about the centre, but failing to illuminate corners that were soaked with darkness. Despite the bright day and the rounded-off plaster, there was still a tension to the house, as though the air itself were sprung. She walked upstairs, and the unease only deepened. On the edge of the top step were a couple of dried petals, a faded version of the virulent yellow of the roses that grew just in front of the old number 3. She hated those roses and wondered how they had got there. The narrow staircase of what had been the old Mrs Crale's house was lit by a skylight, but the sun fell only in silvery slivers on uneven walls, and a pang that Rowena barely recognised as guilt flittered past her near little Bobby's room, which was where Mrs Crale had slept. It was there that all the shadows of these crooked cottages condensed, congealed even, and Rowena sped past, harried by a sadness or a worry she couldn't remember.

Their plan to move Mrs Crale had not been so very bad, she thought, trying to comfort herself. She had been a danger to herself. But Scotland was so far away. It was the distance, as much as anything, that had so filled her with hopelessness and had had such painful consequences. *And they had wanted her house.* It was what Evangeline perpetually threw at them. In moments of honesty, she couldn't disagree. How much had this influenced their decision to send her to her goddaughter? It had been a mistake. She held her head in her hands and stood there in the passage.

'Mummmmmmyyyyyy,' called Bob from his bed, so she had to go into his room. She sped through the pool of ill ease, and kissed Bobby's warm little cheek.

'I 'ear dem again!' he said.

'Hear what, my darling?' she said, stroking his hair.

'Foots. Cats.'

'What was it you heard?' she murmured.

'Um, dunno! Robots! Cats!'

'Oh, darling,' said Rowena, smiling. 'And what were the cats doing?' she said in a colluding tease.

'Kit sounds. I like 'em.'

'What sound does a cat make?'

'Miaow.'

She kissed him again, then remembered the cat's urine smell. 'Is that what you hear?'

'Quack quack! Bow wow. Moo moo,' he said, and she smiled in relief.

'My silly Bobby. My Bobbit! Come down for your orange juice now.'

Downstairs, Pollard was smoothing a section of plaster. Clutching Bob's hand, Rowena gazed around the room, her mind trying out her pallet of colours, although if Douglas said they could afford it, she would use a basket-weave wallpaper. Their house would soon be smarter, lighter, cleaner, and they could begin to live as a civilised family. Bob walked away, and she was aware of him behind her as she discussed decorations with Pollard, but she turned and he wasn't there. He was playing in the corner with Pollard's bucket.

5

'Have you seen that astonishing-looking child next door?' said Lana Dangerfield to her husband.

'That nineteenth-century ghost girl, you mean? I rather admire her spirit. She has the villagers in jitters.'

'No no. I think she looks a fright. The poor mother should be firmer. I meant, the fair-haired one. The beauty.'

'I find her creepy. She looks like one of those dolls in a horror film.'

'Oh, Greg, you always *must* be perverse.'

He winked. 'You think so?'

Smiling to himself, he went off to the shrubbery at the end of the garden, and there was Rowena Crale.

'Good afternoon,' he said.

She jumped.

'I'm sorry. I didn't mean to startle you. How were those silly wives the other evening?'

'Who? Oh. Yes. They were welcoming. Lana is — how nice to have her as a neighbour.'

She pulled in her stomach as she spoke, despairing over her baby flab. She had been told by the Wives' Association about the slimmers' club that met in the church hall, but in the meantime, she had seen an advertisement she was hiding in her underwear drawer for a remarkable girdle that sent electric impulses to the fat cells. The idea terrified her even as it offered hope.

'Get away from all that,' said Gregory. 'I'll show you round the power station. We can drive over there.'

'Can we?' said Rowena, tilting her face to the ground to hide her colour. To her consternation, she felt light-headed, out there in the sun.

'We'll nip over there in the MG. She runs like a tiger, you know, all purr and power. You should see the airfield as well. Monday? I can show you the very core — the reactor. One day our whole country will run on a few of them.'

'Yes,' said Rowena. 'I will ask Douglas,' she said, because she was flustered.

Gregory paused a beat. 'For permission to visit a

chap's workplace?' he said in jocular tones. 'You don't need a licence for that. When it comes to flying, it's a different matter.'

'Oh,' she said. 'I—'

'Think about it,' he said, and he grinned at her through the laurel, so that she thought in that moment he resembled Clark Gable as Rhett Butler, though he didn't. She watched his back as he walked across his lawn, the arrangement and movement of his muscles, and willed him to turn. Just as she was about to give up, he did. She felt giddy. She slapped her hand, as though she herself were one of her children. Baby Caroline was crying, and the sound was a mere backdrop.

The neglect and sprawl of the Pollards' house was remarkable to the children who visited it. Most of the land had been sold off, but the house the Pollards rented came with a sizeable section of disused farm containing many outbuildings, a row of empty cattle pens, two nettle-run fields, and an old haystack that still sagged in a barn. On Saturday, Bob stayed at home, but the four Crale girls arrived, the perambulator stalling and jiggling over the path to the house, baby Caroline sleeping through it all.

'Welcome,' said Pollard. 'Have a cat,' he said as a pair of them trotted up to Eva and thumped their bodies against her skirts. 'Each can have a cat. We got plenty.'

'Have a cat, Pollard? To keep?' said Eva. Excitement she barely dared trust bubbled inside her.

'If your mother and father let you. Each. The baby too. Keep 'em here if you prefer.'

'Thank *you*,' breathed Eva.

'They're so big,' Jennifer murmured.

'Some of them is mated from wild cats, brought from the mountains,' he said.

The twins spent the afternoon dipping among the dock leaves in their pastel-checked frocks, one green, one pink, choosing cats to own and keep at the Pollards' while Eva, who had selected a scruffy white, explored the upstairs of the house and Mrs Pollard took over baby Caroline. The girls ran wild, eating cakes and climbing the haystack, which contained sulphurous abandoned eggs and rat holes to collapse into. There were barn lofts, sheds and caravans, an old farmer's office, an abandoned grain store and dangerous machinery. A broken tree house could be accessed by a rope. Freddie was stuck up there, Eva claimed. 'I'll fetch 'im down,' said Pollard matter-of-factly.

Upstairs in the house, room led into room, largely unused. There were rows of beds beneath a dipping ceiling.

'Whose are these?' said Eva.

'Anyone's who wants. Always a bed for you.'

'Truly?' said Eva, her slow husky voice lifting. No adult had ever been so kind to her, ever approved of her so much or treated her like the others. Love for Pollard bubbled up like a thick, warm substance.

'Course. You can escape that mad school, help with the nippers, bed down here. The missus would be pleased.'

'Oh, *thank you.*'

'This is yours,' said Pollard, gesturing at one of the sagging iron beds covered in candlewick, in dusty eiderdowns and tartan blankets. 'Or this. Or this. When you want to skip over. I cook up my own breakfast. We'll have one now.'

'But Pollard, it's *after*noon!'

'No matter,' he said.

He fried a pan of eggs and bacon in his shed while whistling along to Radio Luxembourg and offering the girls cigarettes as they waited in a fug of smoke and bacon fat.

'This is your pew,' he said to Eva, removing a pile of tabloids from a chair.

I am his favourite, thought Eva. She felt light-headed, almost dizzy, with astonished excitement.

'Let me paint the young miss,' said Pollard, poking a paintbrush behind his ear before he handed out plates with one hand and smoked with the other. And suddenly, Jennifer Crale was standing on a stool by the window playing with her plaits, the afternoon light catching her famed dimple through smeared glass, while Eva stood, frozen, in a corner.

Finally, it is all better, thought Rowena once the splendid wallpaper was up and sitting flush with the new arch, replacing the disgraceful dated pattern. Her previous fears were the products of her usual overheated imagination, she thought, not able to let them go entirely, but grateful that this was so.

The damp was quite at bay; the floorboards on the landing were about to be replaced. It was a new start. That unnerving smell of perfume seemed to have gone with the wall. She drank some of the Chianti that the neighbours Gregory and Lana Dangerfield had brought over as a friendly gesture, and she pictured Greg standing near her to pour her more, and a tiny shiver went up her. They were merry, half-camping, a candle pushed into a Mateus Rosé bottle and the children in bed, even the exacting Douglas relaxed, his tie looped over a door handle.

Greg yawned. He rested his head on the back of the chair. 'I still don't understand the source of that damp,' he said. 'In fact, there's something I can't quite work out altogether if you ask me, Douglas. Your fourth skylight.'

'Eh?'

'Step outside, old chap,' said Greg, and they both stumbled as they rose and laughed.

They stood across the lane on the edge of the green, illuminated by the old-fashioned street lamps and the enchanting blue-green-red lights from the pub, and Greg pointed at the roof.

'That's the one at the top of the front staircase,' said Douglas.

'No, it is not, my good man. That one faces the back. Think about it. The window below is in one of the bedrooms, and the other visible skylight is I believe a bathroom?'

'Yes, bedrooms in the eaves,' said Douglas. 'They've eked out rooms over time in these cottages. There's only a very shallow loft.'

'Yes, yes,' said Greg impatiently. 'But I looked around when you had your wall problem. That tiny window high up in the roof is not accounted for.'

'Must be in the loft,' said Douglas. 'For God's sake, let's get another drink.'

'I think not, if I may be so bold,' said Gregory, hiccupping, and he went back in.

Rowena sat very still as Greg climbed the stairs, silhouetted as he disappeared from sight.

He re-emerged, setting up a creaking on the small staircase.

'I may be three sheets to the wind, and the corner throws the floor plan, but I surmise there's a space not accounted for – some of the layout is puzzling. Quite illogical. You could be using it, even if for storage.'

'Oh, who knows in these higgledy-piggledy little places,' said Rowena. 'This is the most quaint, queer sprawl, all steps and, and – corners, ang-angles.'

Douglas glanced at her and took her glass away. She walked carefully to the kitchen and drank some water, pressing her face to the window and gazing at the black laurel.

After a while, Greg came in as she had hoped he might; as she had dreaded he might.

'I'm terribly squiffy,' he said in a quick murmur, picking up a glass and putting it down. 'There are so many words I could say to you—'

'You must not,' said Rowena, colouring, and that night she kissed Douglas for the first time since the baby was born. She felt as though she would be eaten alive, and she pulled away quickly and pretended she could hear Caroline cry.

In the morning, Rowena woke to the baby's cries with an ache clinging to her forehead, but the light sprang on to the walls and she remembered her new large room downstairs and Gregory Dangerfield's words in her ear, and the hangover rocked inside her head as she rose, but still she sang a few notes as she went to lift baby Caroline to smell her nappy. Eva was, as so often, out of the house, and Douglas had already left for work.

'Cat, friends,' said Bob. He made bubbles with his spit as Rowena fetched his clothes.

Rowena heard a mewing as she descended the stairs, and she jumped and looked behind her, where the sound seemed to be coming from, but when she glanced out of the thick-set little window that faced the green there was a black-and-white cat among the geraniums on the window box. The smart new basket-weave wallpaper smiled at her. She loved it: she was modern, she was a Londoner. After all those years in London she would never return to her provincial identity, and it was somehow *humorous* to decorate a low-ceilinged cottage thus.

Wallpaper paste and old cigarettes scented the air. She gazed at the quirky white-and-yellow pattern, taking it all in, and there was a stain like a floater on her vision. She tried to resist it, lifting her eyes slowly and persuading herself it was a shadow. She looked again. A small stain had appeared where wall met ceiling, and she closed her eyes and stood very still and kept them closed. She pictured the old lady who had lived here, and starved herself here. This was an old lady's house. An old lady called Evangeline Crale.

Guilt spread through her mind, like the damp: a stain of it.

6

'Where is Eva?' said Rowena.

'I don't know, Mummy,' said the dark twin Rosemary.

'She keeps disappearing,' said Rowena. 'Even more than she usually does.'

Jennifer arrived at the door. 'She goes to Mr Pollard's,' she said.

'I need to speak to that man,' barked Douglas. 'Get him on the phone for me, Ro.'

'Mummy, a lady gave me this card,' said Jennifer, and Rowena glanced at a woman's name and number while she importuned Pollard to come straight round.

'I shall ask the actress, Lally Lyn, about this,' she said uncertainly, then held the card out to Douglas, who frowned.

'Film people nonsense?' he said. 'Find out exactly what they want first.'

'Yes, darling,' said Rowena, catching sight of Jennifer, who had her hair loose, its plait-bobbled ashes and golds jumping with light, and she knew very well what they wanted, and mad pride reared inside her even as good sense cautioned her. She thought she saw a shadow of Evangeline by the door. 'Eva?' she called out, but it was too late.

Jennifer leaned on the arch: the symmetry against the white-and-yellow basket-weave a perfectly composed portrait, except the stain above was growing, a tea-coloured exudation with angry borders the colour of old blood, quite wrecking the expensive wallpaper.

'Oh, Douglas,' she said weakly, glancing up.

'Absurd!' he barked. 'I'll give Pollard a drubbing. He needs to investigate the roof. The plumbing. I'll dock that bloody roll of wallpaper from his wages and he can hang it again.'

Rowena jumped slightly as she recognised the figure of Gregory Dangerfield passing the window in his cricketing clothes. He didn't look in at her. A flash of profile, of a distinctive, almost school-boyish, curve of hair at his temple. She wanted to see the dark brown eyes that seemed to contain such soulfulness in his rare quieter moments. She cleared up, and found herself working out what time he might come back, and whether she could stroll to the village shop wheeling Caroline past the game. She couldn't do these things, though. She was a married woman.

'Pollard, what the hell's the meaning of this continued damp?' snapped Douglas when Pollard arrived. 'Apparently there may be some space up there not being used? Behind a wall? It must be coming from there, for heaven's sakes.'

Pollard hesitated, then spoke, impassive as ever. 'An old water tank,' he said. 'I found it. You got a different system now.'

'Yes?' Douglas waited.

'That's it,' said Pollard.

'For goodness' sakes, why didn't you remove the thing?'

'Rusted in, and wouldn't fit down the staircase, sir.'

'Well, how the hell did it get *in*?'

'They's changed the architecture many times over years. That won't be the original staircase, sir. You can see ghosts of others. Look at that wall.'

He pointed. A faint door-shaped outline was visible through the plaster. At the other end of the room, off the hall, a couple of tiled steps led to nothing.

Douglas was momentarily silenced.

'Lintels poking through upstairs, too,' said Pollard.

'Show me.'

'Door once there,' said Pollard, pointing on the landing. 'That bit of beam sawn off. Lintels showing. Like bodies under the sand. After time and tide, they bulge through.'

'All right, Pollard. Enough,' said Douglas. 'So what did you do with the space that encloses the old water tank?'

'Airing cupboard, sir. Tank was in an old airing cupboard. Small. Nothing much. Took up all the space.'

Douglas looked blank.

'Continued the tonguey groove up there over it, sir,' said Pollard, pointing at the wall that met a corner outside Bob's room. 'Nothing else to be done.'

'Well, you will have to investigate everywhere for the source of this damp.'

'I have, sir. Water tank was empty, not plumbed in. Nothing is causing it.'

'Then I'll get someone else in to find it! Get back home, Pollard, and be quick about it.'

'Where is Eva?' said Rowena as the sun sank in honeyed shadows over the green, geese flying overhead.

No one knew.

'Don't worry about her, Mummy,' said Rosemary.

'I do, though,' said Rowena. She laid out her children's baked beans and wondered what Gregory Dangerfield was doing. Mrs Pollard, who ran some sort of kindergarten, had offered to have baby Caroline the next day, and perhaps he would ask her again to visit the power station, though she had been discouraging and he hadn't repeated the offer. The shadows cooled and lengthened; she heard a cheer rising from the cricket field. The men would be off drinking and toasting each other now. The dank dark middle of the room where the wall had stood before it died seemed to clench momentarily in a passing coldness, and there at the end of the arch where it met the wall that faced the green was the shadow of liquid pressing up between the tiles, making them quite loose.

'No,' murmured Rowena. 'No, please.' She had a sense that she couldn't control this. She saw herself running, warding back damp, soaking up liquid, but then new damp would push up like mushrooms somewhere else.

The children were watching *The Saint* and chattering in the dining room, Douglas reading his newspaper. She felt the need, again, to count the children. She knelt down and pressed her fingers against several tiles, which had loosened themselves and gave slightly beneath her hand, little springs of water appearing in rectangles. She laid her head against the edge of the arch, but it was cold, even covered in wallpaper. At that moment, she smelled the perfume again. It was the old Evangeline Crale's. 'Please,' she said. 'Please.

'I just need a walk,' she called to Douglas. 'Just one turn round the green.'

She let herself out of the door and breathed in the freshly rinsed air. Several villagers were out walking in the late sunshine, and nodded to her. There was another new family who had moved in just before the Crales; they were friendly and had already asked the older girls round to play. Rowena chatted briefly to them, then the daughter lingered as her parents walked to the pond.

'Mrs Crale,' she said, almost bobbing, politely. 'Please, who is the face looking out of your window?'

Rowena paused. 'What do you mean?' she said.

'The lady.'

Rowena frowned.

'She wears pale clothes.'

Rowena paused again. 'It must be Eva?' she said eventually. 'She's older than you, but she's not a lady!'

The girl shook her head. 'Thank you,' she said hesitantly, almost bobbed again, and ran after her parents.

✶

Eva was absent, as she increasingly was.

'She has gone to help my missus as I understand, Mrs Crale,' Pollard said to Rowena the next evening. 'If that is acceptable to you.'

'Yes,' said Rowena after a moment of contemplation, encouraged by this unprecedented adult acceptance of poor Eva.

Rowena had arranged that Mrs Pollard was to have baby Caroline for three hours each weekday morning while she herself supervised the decorating and cooked for the family, for there had been too much tinned soup and sardines. She was reading recipes at night and was determined to make more of an effort.

The twins Rosemary and Jennifer set off with baby Caroline in her pram, out along the narrowing lanes at the top of the village, then west across the track leading over empty fields to the Pollards' house, Brinden.

'My dears,' said Mrs Pollard, standing in her porch in a lemon-yellow housecoat and clasping Jennifer and Rosemary, one hand each. Her wide blue eyes in her round childish face widened until she was a series of circles, her voice a scoop of meringue. 'I only saw you playing from a distance last time, though we are looking after your cats, Ginger and Rosie. Dear Evangeline has been telling me all about you.'

She looked at them as she spoke, studying them for the first time, smiling at dark stolid Rosemary, then turning to Jennifer.

She gazed, stared at her, her mouth still; then her eyes moistened momentarily. 'Why,' she said, 'I – I – Mr Pollard had told me about you – girls – all your family – but – I didn't know—' She blinked and composed herself. 'Come in, dears. Bring dear Caroline into my little family of babies and then we big girls will pour ourselves out some Ribena.'

'Thank you,' said Rosemary and wheeled the pram round the side of the house into the back garden, where her cat Rosie sat on a wall.

'Look what I have for you!' said Mrs Pollard, holding two yoghurt pots. 'Ski with real fruit. You must try it, girls.'

Jennifer's sapphire irises, the saturated Technicolor intensity of her colouring, seemed to pull the light of the room to her, but she ate unawares and licked the yoghurt off her raspberry-shaded top lip and said thank you prettily, her spaced pearl teeth gleaming white as she smiled.

'Where is Eva?' said Rosemary.

'Why, looking after the babies as ever,' said Mrs Pollard.

*

Evangeline waited in the fields in her grey serge for Mr Pollard to emerge from his day's work, then she skipped along the lane and caught his arm, and she looked up at him and smiled, and they chatted together about her pregnant cat Meribell, and about the many many places in the house, in the farm, in the outbuildings, to conceal oneself in a game of hide-and-seek.

'You don't know the half of them,' said Pollard cheerfully, 'though you're the sharpest of your sisters. I'll plant some of them Caramacs you like in the nooks and crannies, and if you find them, you shall gobble them.'

He laughed, and Eva laughed with delight, and gave him a kiss on his dusty cheek. His face was like an almost-handsome boy's, delicate and triangular but weathered, with tilted bright eyes and a curved smile.

'You don't mind about *any*thing, do you?' she said. 'No rules here, no punishments, no – normal grown-ups.'

'A treasure hunt before we get to hide-and-seek,' he said. 'Don't forget there's up the trees. Platforms. Bet you ain't found the animal shelters behind the haystack yet.'

'Oh, Brinden is the most fun place in *the* world,' she said.

*

At home, Rowena crept up the stairs. She was nervous there. As the cottages merged, 2 and 3 The Farings became a larger house, all bewildering shapes and angles, yet there was something about the half that had belonged to Mrs Crale that retained a sadness, a dull whine of discomfort. She would not even look at the stain, at the pool of water in the corner, she decided: Pollard would fix it all, once he had knocked a doorway through the two cottages upstairs, ripped out the old kitchen on Mrs Crale's side, and completed the papering and painting of bedrooms. And if he was incapable of sourcing and remedying the damp, Douglas said, he would bring up a more qualified fellow from town.

Today the house smelled of Milton disinfectant, of foods failing in the heat, the meat swelling, the Cheddar sweating in beads. The old fly papers Rowena couldn't reach hung completely still by the open window, the insect fragments on them desiccated. She now acknowledged to herself that she didn't like going up the stairs on Mrs Crale's side, the landing outside Bob's room uneasy in its varying light. She had noticed that Jennifer didn't like those stairs either; she would ask again whether it was possible to remove the staircase altogether once the top floors were knocked through, so they could go up through the back steps only.

Bob slept, and Rowena had to traverse the pool of sadness to wake him. Sounds came to her: voices, words, sentences half-caught. It was Eva, who must have returned from wherever she had gone to. Wasn't she supposed to have grown out of imaginary friends at this age, she wondered? Ridiculously, Rowena almost felt she herself knew Freddie by now. She frowned. Perhaps Eva would make friends at Ragdell Place. Rowena pictured a straggle of unfortunates, grimacing and staring, poking, pinching, wetting, and she shuddered, and regretted, for a moment, putting her down for that school, because even though Eva's behaviour and appearance were becoming more extreme with age, she kept more and more to herself. She was, as she reminded Douglas, little trouble in some ways. 'She is a full-blown embarrassment,' snapped Douglas.

A cacophony of murmuring made her shudder, and she woke Bob and hurried downstairs with his warm protesting body in her arms.

7

On Thursday, Evangeline stood scowling in the dazzle of sunshine on the set of the film *Blush* as the crew shot a scene on location in Crowsley Beck. She hung around all morning, hoping to be noticed.

'*There* she is,' said Rowena, approaching. She tried to draw Eva towards her for a hug to which she submitted stiffly.

'She just likes being on her own, Mummy,' said Rosemary solemnly. 'She has Freddie.'

'Yes, darling,' said Rowena, drawing in her breath as Jennifer was accompanied on to the green, followed by the actress Lally Lyn who had requested that the lovely Miss Crale play the role of her young sister.

'Looks more like her daughter,' Gregory muttered to Rowena a little too audibly.

Rowena tried not to smile. The daring of this man was meat and drink to her. She wanted to stay outside, lapping it up, away from the shadows. She willed him to touch her, anywhere – brush her arm, her shoulder – but he didn't.

'Keeping it all on home territory, darling,' said Lally in an aside to Rowena. 'The only time in my *life*! Some of the other scenes will be shot in bloody Cornwall. Isn't she angelic?'

Jennifer Crale stood bolt upright on the green with her short skirt protruding starchily, her plaits looped Heidi-style, each strand corn-sheaf regular, and lights and reflectors trained on her even on this most glaring of summer days, while Lally Lyn wore a blonde beehive hairpiece falling into long tendrils by her ears that made her look top heavy, her lipstick like hoar frost. A make-up artist dashed over and ran a large brush over Jennifer's cheeks.

After half an hour during which various departments worked around her, the clapper board shut and Jennifer spoke. 'Yes, I shall, Gloria,' was her only line in the one scene in which she was to appear. She was barely audible.

She said her line a dozen or so more times. 'Cut,' shouted the director.

Lally Lyn whispered something reassuring in her ear and she smiled.

She tried again.

'Could the audience – would you mind? – scooting off?' called an assistant director, wiping his forehead, and the loiterers slowly moved away.

Village children were encouraged to keep playing in the background while Lally and Jennifer spoke: Rosemary and Bob played catch with Peter and Jane and the post office children. Eva joined them, wearing laddered stockings on this hot day, a pinafore and velvet ribbon, and she blew her nose on her grandmother's lace handkerchief. With her colourless hair, she looked like a drab spirit among the healthy rosy children in their bright skirts and shorts.

'Girl in apron,' called out the first assistant director. 'Could you please get yourself out of the shot.'

Eva ignored him and carried on playing. 'Catch!' she called to Bob, then to Freddie.

'The girl in the white dress and grey apron, we are catching you on camera,' called the first assistant director on a loudhailer, and Eva stiffened. She heard laughter. She stared at the film set. Her beautiful sister stood in the middle like a glorious statue bathed in heavenly light. Eva's face seemed to burn. In her head, she was there, there shining instead of Jennifer. There and normal and loved and praised. She could say that stupid line. She clutched her grandmother's dress, her link with her, and wondered whether she might combust. She glanced at one of the windows in her house.

'I want to *play* with the others,' she said to the assistant director who strode over to her.

'Not in that get-up. Sorry, lovey.'

'I should like to *be* in the film.'

The assistant director's mouth twitched. 'Sorry, lovey, you haven't got the right look,' he said.

Eva stayed still. The assistant director gestured to a colleague who strode over, and they each took an arm and hauled her off the grass.

'Grandmamma,' she said, looking at her home again, that picture-pretty cottage dozing on a village green. It had been cowed, violated, but the sun glanced off a skylight and at the sight of that, the sign of it, she was resolved.

Rowena went upstairs to tidy some sheets, a job she had been putting off, because whatever she told herself, she simply didn't like going up on that side of the house. Bob's room was the problem. It was still, in her mind, the bedroom of old Evangeline Crale. It was where she had starved herself. Rowena shuddered quite violently.

In the face of Eva's fury, Rowena could barely think about it; yet for all her dismissal, guilt gathered there, as stagnant, sour-edged and undeniably present as the pool of water downstairs. What Rowena always pictured as she lay stroking Bob to sleep was Mrs Crale as she had been when a neighbour had visited her, her head turned to the wall, her eyes close up to the daffodil-print paper that still lined the room. As Rowena lay there kissing little Bob, she gazed at the yellows that slightly overshot their brown outlines and bled into the chalk background. Those cataract-clouded blue eyes in porcelain-delicate skin had studied the same patterns. Rowena could almost smell Mrs Crale there as she willed her life to seep away: her skin, her saliva and tears impregnating the faintly worn wallpaper by the bed. Would she find white *hairs* if she looked on the floor, she wondered, and shuddered.

Rowena sped past the door now, and into the comfort of sunlight in the room baby Caroline shared with Eva, when Eva, who had been a semi-nocturnal creature even from the beginning, was ever there. Caroline didn't stir. Her mouth was open, dribble emerging from it in a shining trickle. Rowena watched her. For a few moments, she didn't breathe. Rowena snatched her up, suddenly fearing for her children in ways she couldn't specify, and hugged her hard to her, burying her nose, almost snorting the milk-warm scent of her skin, because there was the faintest undertow of the perfume that bothered her in the room, emerging from Eva's trunk of clothes. She pressed against Caroline's hot cheek so hard that the baby began to cry, bawling loudly with life and protest that destroyed the skeins of scent and decay. She should not, could not, be up here on her own, thought Rowena, and called out quite urgently to Bob, who was on the green outside, to come home. Jennifer was still standing there under a beam of light that was like her own sun.

Bob bounced in holding Rosemary's hand, and Rowena kissed them both and sat them down for their orange juice.

Later, when the church clock struck six, she went by herself and stood at the gate, breathing in the still-hot air. There was a boy behind her, needing her. No, there wasn't, she thought impatiently. But there was a smell, like ice lollies; ice lolly warmed on skin. She made herself turn. This was all Eva's doing. The infernal Freddie creature she insisted on. The film people were packing up, and the trickle of the stream across the green was just audible, comforting after the North Circular, the ducks circling the pond. She stood and watched, sensing that life held far more than was apparent within the dozing confines of Crowsley Beck. New excitement was beginning to take hold of her through the fug of baby-feeding sleepless nights, just as new anxieties were unexpectedly gripping and shaking her mind.

The MG appeared through the arc of horse chestnuts leading into the village and crunched to a halt on the lane.

'Got you a viewing of the rushes,' said Gregory, letting his dog leap out.

'I'm sorry?'

'Come and see the rushes tomorrow. The dailies. What they filmed today.'

'Already tomorrow?' said Rowena, bemused.

'Oh, they put it in the bath overnight and the important bods view a rough cut. Lally knows the producer – rather well, if you ask me – and I persuaded her to get us sneaked in to the viewing theatre as a favour, to have a squint at today's footage.'

'But . . . Douglas?' Rowena murmured, looking at her toes.

Gregory hesitated. 'He can come along too, I'm sure. It'll be only a few seconds, you understand. Who'll be left with the brats?'

'We have no sitter yet.'

'I'll send ours over. Mother of the star, of course you must come along. A rare opportunity.'

'She has four words,' said Rowena, noticing that she argued with Gregory or contradicted him by rote, when she wanted to do quite the opposite.

'I'll pick you up at eight. Or you and old Douglas. Then we'll bowl over to Elstree.'

'I – Greg—'

'Come on, it'll be fun. It'll be a Friday night, so Lally says they might get up a bit of a party.'

'The Pollards want you to visit again,' said Eva to Jennifer in a low monotone. 'You are *wanted* at Brinden.'

'Oh,' said Jennifer. 'All right.'

She gave a slight smile, and it was that smile that made Eva want to scream close to her face.

The smoke was so thick in the screening room, Rowena blinked. She coughed, intimidated by these people who were alien to her, a world apart: a planet of louche ease, hardness, success. 'Join them,' said Gregory, and she took one of his Stuyvesants. She was trying to get the taste back for smoking, because her London friends had unanimously declared it kept them trim. She felt her stomach again surreptitiously as she sat, and held it in for Gregory, and wondered whether Douglas would stray before she could force herself to make love with him again, because after all, who wanted to be tied to a frigid dairy cow? She tensed her stomach even harder, and pulled in her cheeks.

'Relax,' whispered Gregory. 'You are beautiful,' he said, as though reading her mind. He beckoned the director, who ignored him. 'Prannet,' Gregory muttered, then hailed him loudly and called out his name. He came over.

Gregory held out his hand. 'Friends of Miss Lyn,' he said lazily. 'Mother of the kid actress is here too. Where's a bloke to get a drink? Ah, thank you.'

He poured Rowena and himself a large cup of the red wine someone had brought in. He was the perfect gentleman, thought Rowena. He looked after her. He strolled over to the table where the director stood, grabbed a bottle and refilled her cup, and yet, sitting beside her he didn't touch her and he said nothing further of a flattering nature. He chatted to her and to others around them, discussing the film, his attention equally shared: she did not have to resist him, which perversely made her want him to flirt with her. Lally Lyn arrived in a houndstooth skirt that was so short, Rowena gasped to herself. 'Miss Lyn has forgotten to attend her wardrobe fitting,' Gregory announced, and Lally paused, wide-eyed, then laughed loudly.

There were many delays, much cursing, tension and cynical joking. I am quite, quite gone, thought Rowena, fuzzily, and she wanted to lean against Gregory, but he was talking to the editor. He returned to his seat, grinned at her, and she sat back in delectable anticipation as the film rolled. It was a black-and-white picture, a small British production, and the green seemed barrel shaped and quaint, fringed by over-dark elms. There stood Jennifer, hands held in front of her as she listened and nodded at Lally Lyn's animated importuning. Rowena tried to deny it to herself, but Jennifer looked puzzlingly ordinary. The camera tightened in on her as she said her one line. In truth, she was a disappointment. The lighting, or the celluloid process itself, somehow failed to capture the breathtaking aspect of her physiognomy. In fact, she looked almost strange, a little disturbing, the eyes that were so glitteringly kingfisher in real life like an empty glare. Rosemary and Bob were just recognisable in the background with other village children.

'Jolly good,' whispered Gregory without conviction.

The camera panned to the cottages alongside the green and Rowena felt the satisfying swoop of familiarity as real life played back to her, and then she thought she saw something. She stared, and blinked. There was a face in a roof window of her house. It had gone. She must have imagined it, she thought; must have put together shadows to make features.

The minutes of film juddered to a halt.

'You'll now see endless takes of the same scene,' whispered Gregory, and Rowena nodded and concentrated. She couldn't blink. She didn't even breathe. And there, as the camera panned swiftly over the cottages beside the green, there was a face in a skylight of The Farings. In its fleetingness she could not be entirely certain – such a tiny detail that no one else would have seen it – but it seemed to her, in a fragment of a second, that the film had caught a face in the shadows of the window, a head in ruffles of lace, in a lace cap, the eyes staring out over the horizon. The crying wrinkled face came back to her, the haunted eyes of homelessness, but of course it was Eva, dressed in her grandmother's clothes. She looks so like her, Rowena thought miserably, and she leaned against Gregory.

'What's this?' said Gregory, glancing down at her with an amused expression, then he put his arm around her.

'I – I feel a little faint,' she said.

'Just watch the last takes and we can leave,' he murmured.

The same scene ran again, Jennifer delivering her line with no more conviction. Rowena stared at the screen. This time, the face wasn't there. She frowned. She watched the next take, and all that followed, and the face was no longer in the window.

'Can you take me out, Gregory?' she said.

'Mrs Crale does not feel well,' he announced, standing. 'It's an oven in here. Splendid job, chaps. Can't wait to see snoozing Crowsley Beck on the silver screen.'

'I feel sick,' said Rowena, leaning against Gregory in the cooling air.

He held her arm. He hesitated, then pulled her against him so she could feel the warmth of his skin beneath his shirt. She quivered. The wine rolled inside her. She wanted life, hot dark urgent life, not guilt, this endless growing guilt.

'You can,' she said.

'I can?' he said playfully, but his voice snagged.

'Yes.'

'Are you sure?' he said earnestly, lifting her chin and looking her in the eye.

She pressed against him, gazing back. He was all dark brows and shaded sockets, his contrasts black and pale silver in the night, like film.

She nodded. 'Yes,' she said.

The damp was oozing up through the tiles again, a pool now catching the moonlight and infusing the room with the breath of brackish water. Rowena hurried past it. Was it a mistake coming here? The thought came at her obliquely, as though it were not her own. She wouldn't countenance it, she thought stoutly. They simply had to be patient. She remembered the dead canary, Mrs Crale's, and almost thought she could smell it as a dank decaying undernote. Its cage was in the side porch, waiting for the Radlett rag-and-bone man. Douglas must have disposed of its body. The damp stain above her – I must face it, face it all down, she thought hectically – was growing and now it started to look faintly avian to her, like the poor shot birds on Mrs Crale's ugly wallpaper, and oh, she had done wrong. She vomited, between the sink and the kitchen floor, and then stood there panting. 'My God,' she said out loud. Her forehead cold; she cleared up, gagging again, and washed herself.

She forced herself up the staircase to check on Bob and Caroline. Was that where Eva hid, then, somewhere in the loft, up here? She glanced at the hatch in the landing ceiling, dimly illuminated. It was barely a loft, Douglas had said: the bedrooms themselves were built into a portion of the roof, so there was only a shallow tent-shaped storage space up there. Was poor Eva crouched in the loft? Rowena didn't want to know. She didn't want to see her strange daughter in her strange Victorian clothes talking to her awful invented friend. She did not. She checked on her little ones, ran down the stairs and back up the other staircase into her own room, and there was Douglas spreadeagled and asleep. 'Sorry,' she murmured. 'Sorry. I'm sorry.'

8

The next day, Pollard knocked through the wall on the upper floor in under two hours, the bricks, lath and plaster succumbing limply to his blows in a settling spray of dust and dirt, as though already defeated.

Jennifer offered to take baby Caroline to Mrs Pollard's. Rowena watched her as she darted all the way round the back to the far staircase to fetch Caroline's sun bonnet from her room. Rosemary stayed at home to draw, Rowena cleared up, and the boy was behind her again. Boy, she wondered? Why had she thought there was a boy? Bob was running around by himself, noticeably energetic in the garden, but she had felt something like a glimmer or a lash on the side of her eye: a knowledge that someone was there. It was as though the air was disturbed.

She drew herself up and dismissed it quite strictly, and Jennifer dashed back into the room with Caroline's little mint-coloured sun bonnet and set off with the perambulator.

Eva had shown Jennifer a new track she had found across the fields behind the stream that they could use when the weather was hot and the mud had all dried, though baby Caroline bounced up and down on groaning springs, asleep or crying. It was faster than going by the lanes round the back of the village.

Eva was already there when Jennifer arrived.

'Why are you here?' she hissed to Jennifer.

'To see Mrs Pollard,' said Jennifer calmly.

Eva glanced at her. There was little else to say. 'Why? *Why?*' she said eventually. 'Do you like Mr *Pollard?*'

'I like them both,' said Jennifer. 'Mrs Pollard's hairdressing salon is starting today in the garden. I am to be her first model girl.'

'Is that what's in that frilly-silly bag you carry? All your hair *ribbons* and brushes?'

'Yes,' said Jennifer, and smiled.

Eva glared at her.

Mrs Pollard's hairdressing salon involved the placing of chairs under a shelter that Mr Pollard had constructed using a canvas stretched across two walls of breeze block. The girls worked hard together heating Mrs Pollard's wiry bob into a temporary smoothness with hair irons that drew a singed smell, then held her fringe back with a velvet headband. It began to spring loose, so they soaked it in hairspray and added rows of kirby grips, concealed by the band. Mrs Pollard sat very stiff all the while, in a sort of trance, her cream voice stilled.

When they had finished, she stirred herself, examined Jennifer's palms and rubbed in some Astral. 'The hairspray will dry them out,' she said. She whisked a wet flannel over Jennifer's face, then patted her cheeks and the tip of her nose with some sun lotion, passing a scoop to Eva without looking at her.

'Stand up nice and straight, my pet,' she said, repositioning Jennifer's shoulders, and went off to fetch some semolina.

'Is it always to be the food Jennifer *likes*?' growled Eva, barely audibly, as Mrs Pollard returned.

Mrs Pollard cast her a glance.

'That baby food Jennifer eats,' said Eva after an awkwardly long pause. Her eyes were glittering. 'Shall she have *some* rusks, then?'

'Now, now, dear,' said Mrs Pollard impassively. Idly, she picked up Jennifer's spoon and held it to her mouth.

A look of disquiet came over Jennifer's face, and she paused, stiffly, then took a mouthful.

'Good girl,' said Mrs Pollard.

Mrs Pollard selected a number of clips, grips and a can of Elnett and teased and lacquered Jennifer's hair into a tall beehive and attached a little bow at its front. She stood back to admire her work. She stared at Jennifer for some time.

'The prettiest girl in the kingdom, who—'

'She *looks* like a woman!' Eva interrupted, with undisguised indignation. 'She looks so tall! *Grown* up almost. Like a lady.'

'Now you're ready for Arthur,' said Mrs Pollard.

'What do you mean?' said Eva.

'For the new painting. Arthur wants to do some photographs first with his Instamatic camera he bought himself earlier in the year. He had a contract to build three shops! And after that, he treated himself. Now, dear, can you walk carefully to the shed? Don't let the heat spoil your do.'

'But – but—' said Eva. 'He is working at our home.'

'He was going to come back. Did you want your hair done too?' said Mrs Pollard casually, looking back.

'Pollard is here?' said Eva. 'He is here?' She squinted.

'Don't screw up your face like that, my dear. It's bad for beauty. Arthur's at work in his shed. Arranging the sheets for behind the chair. He had to prepare a canvas too.'

Mrs Pollard shielded Jennifer with a parasol as she led her round the house, through the cauliflower beds, to the tangled patch of briar and nettle where Pollard's painting shed stood. Cats followed them.

'Make sure you don't get stung,' she said.

'Where*as* I can?' said Eva, jumping on the nettles and stinging herself. She hissed like one of the cats.

'Now, dear,' said Mrs Pollard calmly to her. 'You must put some of my cream on those. Jennifer, keep your chin tilted. We are nearly there. You can have your little nap afterwards.'

'Beautiful,' said Mr Pollard phlegmatically, glancing up at Jennifer. He nodded at Eva, winked at her. 'Sit yourself there on the chair, Jenn'fer.'

'Am I to *stay*?' said Evangeline thickly.

'Course you can,' he said. 'You can wipe me brushes.'

'While she sits there to be pictured and painted, I am to be a slave girl?' said Eva, trembling, so hot she imagined herself bursting into flame.

Jennifer gazed impassively ahead. A small smile played on her lips, as though she were far away. Mrs Pollard watched her, then with her fingertip she applied a little touch of Vaseline she had mixed with lipstick. Jennifer sat there submissively as she did it.

'I hate you,' said Eva to Jennifer in a long, low growl. Jennifer turned her head just slightly. 'I hate you more than you can possibly imagine.'

'If Pollard doesn't sort out this damp by tomorrow, I'm firing him,' said Douglas darkly.

'He did the wall upstairs with no trouble, but yes . . .' said Rowena, letting her hair, which she was wearing loose today, fall over her face as she broke up mince in a pan.

'I'm not sure he's got the ceiling straight, either.'

Rowena said nothing, but she had wondered if she had perceived a faint bulge in the area above the arch between the main rooms. She also worried about where Eva, who hadn't returned with the others, was. She hadn't seen her in the morning either. Setting the potatoes to boil, she muttered something about the washing, and walked out of number 2 into the darkening strip of garden, avoiding the gate on to the green, for she was hiding from Gregory Dangerfield. She was utterly shocked at herself: so shocked, she could not think about their kiss without trembling and panicking. He was her next-door neighbour. He was confident, laissez-faire, outrageous even. What if he told someone?

Who might have been passing in a car through Elstree at night, a beam of headlights circling her face caught pressed against Greg's? She had never *dreamed* she would do such a thing. Douglas's fist – he who had not laid a hand on her – lifted in her mind, and behind him was the face of old Mrs Crale in shock.

Other images leapt at her: the scandal, her running away, gathering her children and running, running from shame and damnation, across the green, Caroline in her arms, Bob dragging on her hand, the twins in front, but where was Evangeline? She had slipped out of the picture. Another one seemed to be there. He flickered into her mind, and she swept him away, impatiently, just as she always dismissed the silly idea of Freddie. Where *was* Evangeline? And how would she make money? A sparse display of qualifications shuffled into place: that Distinction in her School Certificate. Secretarial college. The seventeen friend-packed months as ground staff for BEA, before Douglas Crale arrived and swept her from her desk. Marriage at twenty. She could type, and she could take shorthand. She had had elocution lessons disguised as speech and drama classes in her teens, and she was – she could admit it now, in desperation – considered nice-looking. But five children. Could you feed five children on that, as a shamed woman, an 'A' branded on your forehead? She knew the answer.

She heard a voice and jumped. What if *Lana* Dangerfield caught her in the shadows? Threw a kitchen knife at her? She shrank among the bushes near the house.

She pressed herself against the warm bricks of the cottage wall, barely breathing. Two or three men chatted about the film, inconsequentially, words lost among clear sentences, ragged laughter floating over from the pub, an engine starting. She knew by their delivery that they were part of the crew, and they seemed to be packing up a vehicle outside her gate. She listened for a while, heard snatches of conversation, and then she started to inch her way back towards the kitchen, where the potatoes would be cooked.

'Big family,' said one of them, and Rowena stopped and began to listen again. '. . . had to drag one of them off.'

'. . . messing up the scene . . . don't look alike . . . Lally . . .'

There was more laughter, more noises as equipment was slung into a vehicle.

'Creepy creepy . . .' Laughter. Rowena froze. Anger made her rigid. Leave her alone, she thought, and Evangeline's poor scrawny face came to her. She had looked hungry even as a baby, and yet she would not feed.

'. . . bloody weird . . . it's those eyes. Like a doll . . .'

'. . . zombie doll!'

'. . . creepy eyes. She could have been in that John Wyndham film they made up here.'

Leave my daughter alone, thought Rowena, and she heard more laughter. She turned suddenly and strode to the gate.

'*Shut up* about Eva,' she shouted, just as the van door was being slammed.

'Eva?' said the one in the driver's seat through his open window as he reversed. He looked puzzled. The man beside him said something, and he accelerated forward. 'Bye,' he called, and drove off fast.

'*My daughter,*' she shrieked.

'Rowena!' called Gregory, running down his lawn towards the laurel, and she started and ran back inside the house. As she scraped burnt potatoes from the bottom of the pan without the light on, she saw him in the ilex shadows, searching for her, and she wanted to weep with longing to be held by him, just as she wanted to cry with shame.

'Where is *Eva?*' said Rowena as she cleared up the dishes, straightened her back and sighed.

'She was at Mrs Pollard's this afternoon,' said

Jennifer, and Rowena nodded. Baby Caroline had come back happy and sleepy. Perhaps Eva had stayed there?

When the children were in bed, Rowena tried to read in the new room, the side the lodgers had lived in, where there was no stain. She lay back in the new wicker chair Douglas had let her buy, and admired the orange plastic lampshade on the pendant light. But as she gazed at its amazing tangerine glow, a spot entered the periphery of her vision like a fly. Her scalp tightened. She stayed very still before she made herself look, putting off that moment, preserving happiness. On the arch, that stiff defeated remnant of the wall, there was a small stain on that side of the room too. It began on the ceiling, and made the paper bulge into a small crumbling brown intrusion. There was no escape. The water seeping through the tiles glittered darkly in the other section, just visible from where she sat, and eventually Rowena put down her book and left the room. When will this *end*? she thought with a suppressed sob, and went to check on the children.

Someone was up there, murmuring. An adult voice, a sigh like an exhalation. 'Bob!' she cried, bursting into his room, but he was asleep, and lifted his head only when she ran over to him.

'Hush, hush,' she said to him, and ran into Eva's

room, where there was no one but the baby. She had not expected Eva to be there. The window, she thought for the first time. Here was the window in the roof. It was too high for Eva to have looked out of it, but she must have climbed on a chair or a stool, or dragged her chest over and watched the filming. She felt relieved. Uncertainty about that face nagged at her, but of course it was Eva, dressed as a Victorian. It had been so fleeting, she might even have imagined it in the first place.

There were no more sounds. Walking through the new doorway Pollard had created into the other cottage, she nearly tripped on a step that he had had to build there in the corridor. Rosemary and Jennifer were in their bedrooms, Rosemary reading and Jennifer listening to the little wireless she had received for her birthday.

'I wonder,' said Douglas, returning at nearly midnight from an outing with some work colleagues, reeking of alcohol. 'Perhaps we were too hard on Mother. This was her home and—'

'Don't say that, don't say that,' said Rowena frantically, instant tears springing to her eyes, but he merely grunted in response, lying on her chest with his mouth open, already falling asleep, dribbling like a baby.

She could smell her mother-in-law's perfume

again. She got up and threw the window wider open, gulping air and looking through the moonlit night for Gregory Dangerfield in his large house, willing, willing him to look out at his own garden from a bedroom. In her mind, she climbed down the creeper and flitted barefoot across his lawn towards him, but though she tried to banish her, Mrs Crale chased her, feeble and stumbling.

9

In the morning, the stain was feathering over the basket-weave, its bright sunshine-coloured patterning bulbous with spreading tufts and runnels of damp that ran from the ceiling to the underside of the arch.

'I can't bear this,' Rowena murmured, turning away from it. I don't know what to do, she thought.

Douglas hugged her, cursed under his breath, summoned Pollard and fired him. Pollard nodded and received the news with his usual self-possession. It was as though he held something back; as though he knew something, or was amused.

'There is no cause for that wall and ceiling damp I can establish,' he said. 'Every pipe and coupling, stopcock, all the washers and tanks is checked. The tiles, gutters, the lids. You've got no rads yet on this side. Isn't a referred leak — all the rads on the other side flushed and bled. As for the floor, my thinking is you're on an underground spring and when you took up the old flooring on this side and dug deeper, the earth got too thin. Membrane broke. Plenty o' hidden rivers round here. Trickling, juggling into London and abouts. The Fleet, the Darent, the Colne, the Quaggy—'

'Thank you, Pollard,' said Douglas cursorily, put a day's wages into his hand as a gesture of goodwill since his wife was useful, and went out to drive to the station for work.

'I hope that Mrs Pollard caring for Caroline in the mornings will make up a bit of the loss,' said Rowena, who felt sorry for Pollard, though he seemed to have accepted the news with alacrity and was humming as he cleared his tools with his usual incongruous physical grace.

Soon after he left, two builders from a London firm arrived. 'Just watch them root out that leak,' Douglas told Rowena on the phone. 'It can't be much of a challenge. It's not as though we're living at bloody Knebworth.'

'They do have delightful designs for the breakfast nook,' she said uncertainly.

'These provincials like Pollard can't compare,' said Douglas. 'Though they're half the price.'

She was now able to acknowledge to herself that the ceiling was sagging. The little sections left of the original wall were bleeding and oozing. She ached over the loss of her expensive wallpaper. A new stain seemed to spread in front of her eyes and she still thought she could smell the dead canary among the mould and dirty water. Her guilt and her unease felt overwhelming. She looked back. This wrongness had started when they knocked down the dividing wall. No, it was before that. It was when they had very tentatively raised the idea of moving to Crowsley Beck, misgivings stalling their discussions, justifications sustaining them. Mrs Crale loomed so much larger here, in her very house, than Rowena had ever known she would.

The new builders were dressed in branded overalls, came equipped with various tools that were clearly more sophisticated than any owned by Arthur Pollard, set damp meters about the house, removed the old thermoplastic tiles, and projected an air of hushed capability.

'Where *is* the damp coming from?' said Rowena to Douglas that evening, her wallpaper by now flopping in sections, grey and gritty with mould. She wanted it scraped off, scraped and peeled and scrubbed and burnt.

He paused. 'Damned if I know,' he said, lighting a cigarette. 'Afraid these fellows can't work out the bloody problem yet either, competent though they are. Don't worry, they'll get there.'

The rain blew through the summer as the weeks passed, hurtling down the gutters, gulleys, drains. The green was drenched, the elms bowed. The windows wept. And still it came sheeting down, spilling in. The refurbishments in the number 2 section of the house remained pin bright, cosy, yet exhilaratingly à la mode. But once you stood in the number 3 side, the cottage-hunched shadows clustered and the black reticulated puddle on the floor was growing. Rowena watched, transfixed, the little bubbles and burps of liquid that rose as the rain continued its assault.

A hand touched hers, and there was the smell of grubby warm hair. 'Freddie,' she said instinctively. 'Bob,' she added, because she had to, but Bob was in the next room. She looked down at her own hands. One had touched the other.

Rowena drove baby Caroline to Mrs Pollard's since no one wanted to walk her through the mud of the Brinden lane. The carrycot jumped and slid on the back seat as she accelerated over skidding puddles and loosened stones. Bob chattered beside her. When she got back, the twins were out with their friends and she was alone with little Bob, but there seemed to her to be another child there, in the other room. Had she arranged for a friend's son to come over, she wondered? Had she *forgotten* about someone's young child and left him in the house? She panicked for a fragment of a second. Of course she hadn't, she thought, her heart racing. So why was there that feeling again, of another child in the house? A boy. And where was Eva? She had been absent for too long this time.

Rowena watched the rain, clutching Bob till he protested, and the perfume smell, the *Je Reviens*, came creeping, retreating, progressing, down the stairs. I am afraid of this house, she thought finally. She felt tearful. A house such as this, a lovely house in a perfect village wonderfully close to London had been her fantasy during a decade and more in a box in the suburbs. As a provincial herself – as Douglas would have sniffily called her with her humble-to-middling Hampshire origins – she felt untethered if she was too far from the capital. Crowsley Beck was perfect. Perfect.

But there is something up there, she thought, and even the staircase seemed to seep with an impenetrable sense of shadow that gathered with more determination on the landing and in Bob's room.

Mrs Crale's room, she thought, then stopped herself. She slipped out to look again for the window that she had seen on the film, certain that Gregory would be at the power station. She stood on the green and gazed upwards, but she was puzzled, because there were two windows in the roof, whereas the bedroom only had one. Hadn't Gregory said this in the beginning? She cast her mind back, a warmth, a wistfulness for him returning to her because she hadn't seen him, though she had heard him humming at the end of his garden, whistling, singing snatches of opera even, romantic arias she recognised and knew were for her. She relived their kiss after the screening. Her knees buckled a little.

The other window was where the empty old water tank was, she remembered. She looked again, and for a moment, she thought she saw the faintest passing hint of illumination like a candle that was running out. She stared, but saw nothing more.

She went back and tried to put Bob down to sleep on the sofa, but he reared up in moments, bright-eyed and excited at the change in routine. She steeled herself and took him up the stairs to his room instead, which was so rain-darkened, she thought for a moment she had left the curtains closed. And there was her boy. He smelled of stream water. But Bob was just in front of her, and the

shape, or shadow movement, had been beside her.
'Oh—' she said, and tucked Bob in, patting his
bottom rhythmically, as she had seen other mothers
do, to send him to sleep, to drum away the thought
with normality. She couldn't look behind her.

'Hear!' said Bob suddenly.

'Here?'

'Dem words. Peoples.'

'Oh God,' muttered Rowena. 'People?' she said,
stroking him.

He nodded, grinning.

'Bobby, do you see someone?'

Bob shook his head, his eyes following the rain
shadows on the ceiling.

'Or do you just hear him?'

'Hear dems.'

'But have you *seen* him?' said Rowena.

Bob looked puzzled. 'I plays with Freddie,' he said
eventually, smiling.

Rowena swallowed. She was silent.

'Yes,' she said then, her voice a croak. 'What does
he look like?'

'Boy.'

'So you've seen him?'

Bob screwed up his forehead. To her horror, his
blue eyes – an echo of Jennifer's, but less azure, less
extraordinary – filled with tears. 'I dunno,' he said,

looking at his fat little lace-ups that she had forgotten to remove. He glanced up at her with the expression of fear that appeared on his face when he thought he was about to get into trouble.

'Oh Bobby,' she said stroking him. 'Don't worry. Just tell me — what do you see?'

Bob frowned again. He shook his head.

Rowena paused. 'Never mind, darling,' she said, and she kissed him. 'Go to sleep now.'

Downstairs, there was a shine on the quarry tiles on the other side of the arch, where there was no outside wall.

'It's impossible,' murmured Rowena, sinking down on her knees. The tile was damp. She pressed into it, hard. The one beside it was cold, with the faintest sheen.

But there isn't even rain on this side, she thought. The corner of the room faced an internal wall and then a corridor. She kneeled on her own, shivering in her pale blue summer dress that flared out and returned most of her waist to her, and clouds burst their contents on to her windows, and damp and mould lined her nose, and her mind was rotting with her house.

'Greg,' she said, hearing an engine starting up outside the house behind the sound of the rain, and she ran outside into the downpour, urgency compelling her against her better judgement, but he was driving away from the side of the lane. 'Gregory,' she screamed, rain assailing her mouth, scalp, neck. She began to run, waving, but the car drove off into the arch of trees that led out of the village towards the power station, the aerodrome, the private schools.

She bent over, rain scoring her back, and began to cry. She didn't stop herself. She stood by the Big House for a few seconds, in full potential view of Lana Dangerfield, and the rain met her tears. As she opened her gate, an engine was audible from behind and the MG drew up beside her.

'I saw you just as you were about to disappear from view,' he said, leaping out. 'You silly girl, you're soaked through.'

She allowed him to hurry her through the gate, and he held her in the kitchen, rain puddling beneath her, steam rising from her as she soaked his chest. The idea of the boy in the house now seemed absurd. She looked up at him finally.

He lifted her hand, and kissed it.

'Mrs Crale,' he said.

'Don't call me that,' she said rapidly.

'My darling Rowena.'

She let her breath out.

'Are my eyes like pandas'?'

'Yes.'

'And my hair has all fallen down.'

'Yes.'

'And look at me. Oh God, I am wet through. I am barely seemly.' She covered herself with her hands.

'Yes,' he said. 'And I have never seen you so gorgeous.'

'God. Greg,' she said.

'Why the dickens have you been avoiding me?'

She felt herself blush. 'You know—'

'Yes, I know why,' he said, taking out a cigarette and lighting another for her.

'Lana might see us!' she said, looking up and starting.

'Only if she walks to the bottom of the garden through torrential rain with an ability to see through semi-darkness into an unlit kitchen,' he said, and she laughed, then hiccupped.

'Excuse me.'

'Come out with me tomorrow,' he said.

'Where? Where could I possibly go out with you?'

'To a candlelit restaurant far away from here, in – in Hampstead, in Bond Street – where I can gaze at you and hold your hand and tell you that I never saw anyone like you in Crowsley Beck.'

'I'm not sure that's much competition,' she said, her mouth twitching.

'In all of South Herts!'

She smiled, gave a moue of objection.

'You're the most bewitching creature I ever did see,' he said, his voice breaking up as he said it. 'We need to spend more time together. I will think.'

His words carried her through the afternoon and evening as she nodded and smiled absently at Bob, and then the twins came back from fetching the baby, trailing vast puddles as they wheeled her in. Caroline gurgled, and was fatter and more contented since she had started going to Mrs Pollard's.

'Where is Eva?' said Rowena. How many times did she say that? *Where is Eva?*

The twins shook their heads, spraying rain.

'Hot bath,' murmured Rowena, taking a wet Caroline out of her pram and stripping her down.

Evangeline had gone. Could she say those words? She couldn't. '*Evangeline,*' she called, knowing it was useless. She stood on a stool in Eva and Caroline's room, lifted the window and let the rain tumble on her head in arrows that pelted her. She looked uselessly through the torrents on the green.

She habitually barely saw her own strange daughter, but there were glimpses, sightings, the odd meal taken, nights in her own bed before an early departure. But even the twins were not now reporting seeing her at the Pollards'. She glanced at the clock. She was waiting for the yardarm, she realised.

'Douglas,' she said when he returned from work. 'I don't know where Eva is.'

He made an impatient plosive sound and shrugged, handing her his jacket. 'Who ever does?'

'Yes, but – Yes, but—'

He suddenly leaned over and kissed her, as though remembering you were supposed to kiss your wife when you returned from work; or, she thought, he had caught sight of the anxiety she must be betraying, and he felt a moment of sympathy. He occasionally did.

'She'll come back,' he said. 'She always does.'

'Yes,' she said uncertainly. 'You're right.'

She appraised her husband. He looked the same as he always had, immune to all the changes that were at large in London, Liverpool, Washington, outer space. He was of medium height, a fact that clearly aggrieved him, as there was an air of strutting self-importance to his gait; he held himself as high as possible, his chin tilted in a slight thrust. His mid-brown hair was still sensibly cut, not so different from when he had been at school. The faintest pot belly was forming, visible only in his white shirts.

He was a decent husband, thought Rowena. She loved him.

With Caroline at Mrs Pollard's for a few hours, she had managed to prepare a shrimp mousse. Lana Dangerfield served a starter and a proper dessert every evening, apparently, though Lana Dangerfield had a nanny and a cleaner. Rowena had thought Douglas would be pleased with her effort, but he barely noticed, then cursorily thanked her when she asked him. She raced up between courses to put baby Caroline to bed, and while the chops browned she looked swiftly in Eva's trunk in case there was some unlikely indication of her where-abouts, but all she saw was a scrumpled layer of the terrible clothes, wrinkled and grubby, and she shuddered with distaste, and hated herself for a transient sense of something close to relief that she was not having to bear the social shame of Eva, the stares and puzzled faces. Once the new term started and Eva was secure in Ragdell Place, life would be easier. But in the meantime, where was she?

She ran back through the pool of darkness by Bob's room, and blame emanated from it at her: blame, blame, guilt.

It was picturing that old woman's face turned to the wall in despair that made her want to cry, to curl up and hide; or, on different days, to protest, justify, explain.

But, she thought, she was old; she was ill.

So shouldn't they have looked after her in her own home? Of course they should have. But in the daze of nappies and gripe water that followed Caroline's birth, the idea of caring for a half-demented mother-in-law almost defeated her. Douglas, she noticed, did not appear to shoulder his share of guilt for the painful decline of his own mother, occasionally barking out an ill-considered statement of regret, while Eva was always there to punish her.

'Please, Douglas, can we get rid of that staircase?' she said as she sped back down to the sizzling meat.

He laughed at her. 'You can't just chop out a staircase,' he said. 'My daffy little love.'

'It doesn't feel right.'

'There's no problem with the staircase. Just this goddamn unexplainable leak.' He gestured at the ceiling. 'Use the other stairs if you've taken against these ones.'

They went to bed. Now that Mrs Pollard was feeding Caroline by bottle – and she would secretly use any excuse to get her off the breast – perhaps her former body would return to her.

'Darling,' she said tentatively to Douglas, trying

hard to do her duty, but he had drunk several glasses of whisky after supper, and she turned her head so she couldn't see the determined look in his eye as he gave her a series of amorous embraces that led to nothing.

10

'Look for Eva,' she said the next day to her older girls. 'Please. Tell her to come home if you see her. Doesn't she help with Caroline and the other babies?'

'Yes, Mummy,' said Jennifer.

But there was no sign of her that evening, so the next day, Rowena went to Mrs Pollard's herself. Smoke emerged from the window of a large shed, its wood damp-greened, and thuggish-looking cats mewed.

'Rosie!' cried Rosemary.

'Ginger!' cried Jennifer.

'Come here, my dear,' said Mrs Pollard, crooning with baby Caroline in her arms and stroking Jennifer's head as she passed.

'Has Eva – Evangeline – been here?'

Mrs Pollard looked at her blankly with her saucer-of-milk eyes, her face so plumply smooth, she looked as though she must be faintly retarded.

'She's a helpful girl,' she said.

'Thank you. Yes. Has she been here?'

'Of course.'

'When? When did you last see her?'

'She just left.'

Rowena paused, relieved but puzzled.

'But it's only half past nine,' she said.

Mrs Pollard met her gaze. 'Why yes, Mrs Crale. Evangeline is an early riser.'

'She stayed the night here?'

There was the faintest pause.

'I don't really know, my dear. She may well have. She knows that any room she wants is hers. There's many a bed here.'

'I see,' said Rowena. 'Can you send her home? Next time.'

'As you wish. Of course.'

Rowena paused again. Mrs Pollard was smiling at her placidly, and she suddenly felt reassured and faintly ridiculous for worrying. It was the summer. Eva ran somewhat wild in the school holidays, and the countryside would afford her infinitely more opportunity, but the terms tethered her to more of a routine.

'Eva likes it here, Mummy,' said Rosemary.

'I'm sure she does.'

'She says Freddie is here, dear,' said Mrs Pollard.

Rowena paused for longer. She coloured faintly. 'Well . . . always? Is he always meant to be here?'

'No. Just some nights. At other times, apparently he goes home without her! There now, my dear, Freddie is one child you do *not* have to worry about!' She winked, slightly, from under her bristling fringe.

'Shall we take Caroline round?' said Rowena, and began to wheel her towards the side of the house.

'Oh, come in through the front door, not the long way round,' said Mrs Pollard in her comforting sponge of a voice and led the way through the hall, which featured several telephones from different eras, some with their wires cut; tools, boxes, hooks, old carriage clocks and sacks piled up among out-of-date catalogues and envelopes. 'Excuse the state of it, please, Mrs Crale,' said Mrs Pollard. 'It's all Arthur's flotsam and jetsam. I only usually show visitors my garden, my parlour and my dining room. This way.'

They entered the dining room, where Mr Pollard's bunches of plastic roses sat in vases on doilies all about the sideboards and his Welsh landscapes decorated the chimney breast.

'Very nice,' said Rowena. The sounds of infants drifted through the open window.

She glanced at the other end of the room and gave a gasp. There on the wall was an oil painting of her daughter. Jennifer Crale gazed into the room with eyes so large and intensely blue, she looked almost inhuman: improbably beautiful. Her plaits were caught up in hangman's nooses, their perfect loops like two sides of a bow. She gazed into the room, a dimple on her cheek, the glisten of imminent laughter animating her mouth, and all of life was there ahead of her in her crystalline eyes and in the smile that danced over her expression. Rowena recognised her pink gingham dress with the rick-rack collar, her yellow cardigan, faithfully reproduced. The painting was skilled but wilful, crude and odd, so vast-orbed its subject recalled a Harlequin Waif or an alien doll.

'My . . . that's Jennifer,' she said eventually, torn between pride and a kind of possessive anger.

'It certainly is. Dear Jennifer. Arthur painted her nicely. I hope you'll agree.'

'Yes, yes,' said Rowena, frowning slightly. She was suddenly worried, but tried to reassure herself.

'And I can see where her glorious beauty comes from, my dear,' said Mrs Pollard, glancing at Rowena with a smile from beneath her fringe.

'She doesn't look like me,' said Rowena bluntly.

'No, but the material's all there,' she said. 'It's strange that she doesn't look directly like you. But you're a fine-looking lady, Mrs Crale. And it's a pleasure to make the acquaintance of the Crale family. Come on now, little Caroline.'

Evangeline was not at home when Rowena returned. But the boy was. It was always when she entered the house or another room that she had a faint awareness that someone else was there, somewhere, just in the periphery of her vision or forgotten in a different room. He watched and retreated, followed and waited. It made her count her children in her head, with a plunge of worry for Eva. Bob barely had friends yet, merely alliances fabricated by her and the other mothers in the Wives' Association, a round of teas and cookery afternoons when local women put their vaguely contemporary children together to squabble, then hug goodbye. Was she looking after one of those children? Had she forgotten who was in her charge? She saw the shadow, almost a dandelion seed, floating past the corner of her eye. More often, it was simply an awareness, a nagging of something she had forgotten. Was it really *Freddie* she was imagining? Was her own mind playing tricks, contaminated by Evangeline's? What was Freddie supposed to look like? She would ask Bob again.

She dreaded the moments she put Bob down for his nap after his lunch. She used the staircase in number 2, walking him all the way along the narrow corridors and round the corner to his bedroom at the far end of number 3, but still the sourness was there on the landing, an underlying mouth-coating of mould, urine, protest, as there had been in the wall that had died. No, it hadn't died, she told herself. They had knocked it down. But it had, hadn't it? It had had life to it, in some inexplicable way. It had cried out. Its stiff edges were the crusts of a carcass, and it was still seeping the life blood that it had once had. Today, the perfume lay in fitful drifts over the shadows.

I want to get out of this house, Rowena thought with heart-sinking realisation.

A brief summer downpour hit the village again and someone appeared on the green, a sole figure out in the rain, and Rowena gazed, barely focusing. It was a girl, making her way from behind the war memorial across the grass. She was so thin that she looked barely human, but rather a half-drowned creature, hair plastered, long frock soaked grey beneath a clinging shawl, the day so leached of colour, she appeared as a Victorian waif in a black-and-white photograph. She was holding the hand of a young child. No, she wasn't; she had merely swung her arm near the little bridge that traversed the stream, where children threw sticks. But was it Evangeline? She seemed thinner, noticeably slighter, and grubbier. It was a girl in a long dress and apron: it could only be Evangeline. Rowena felt relief tangled with anger at her disobedience.

Douglas had provided more housekeeping money for increased hours at Mrs Pollard's while the builders were working on the house, to enable Rowena to supervise every aspect of its decoration, and so Evangeline's absence was not as noticeable as it would have been in less busy weeks. The decorating helped Rowena to keep away from Gregory, for she was resolved again, ricocheting between horror that they had kissed and simple fear. The twins reported seeing Evangeline, yet they, especially Jennifer, were vague, and the sightings, by their account, had been brief.

Later in the week, she saw Eva twice through the downstairs window of number 3, but she was yet thinner, and once she turned with an even scrawnier face to look at the house from the green, and Rowena was shocked.

Ignoring the possibility of discovery by Gregory or Lana Dangerfield, she raced out on to the green. 'Eva, Eva, come back home,' she called, but it was dusk, and the shadows were long, the elm shade knotty, and Eva had flickered away. There was a boy there. On the other side of the green. But he too left, down where the stream was.

'Eva, come home and eat,' Rowena called. 'Darling,' she shouted, sounding like a madwoman. '*Evangeline*,' she said.

After a fortnight's work, the builders had made a breakfast nook, complete with delightful red tiles, a wood-effect surface, and a matching red floor. Mrs Crale's old kitchen with its smoking range was turned into a playroom, her pantry into a downstairs lavatory, and the kitchen in the original number 2 had been entirely remodelled. But still the damp oozed, bubbled, crusted. Rowena heard footsteps; she was sure she did, but it was her own poor imagination. Now she was left in the house with Bob, the others playing, a pump chugging, a polythene membrane added, clay air bricks inserted, and the lovely wallpaper entirely ruined.

'Eva has *gone*, do you understand that?' said

Rowena to Douglas later that night. 'She doesn't come home.'

He shrugged reflexively. Then for the first time, he looked worried.

'I'll ring the police station in the morning,' he said.

11

'My daughter has gone,' Rowena said to the doctor, because Douglas had advised her she should make an appointment. She wasn't sleeping, and she was jumping at shadows. Dr Crewe gave her some Librium that would help her, and added a prescription to precipitate the loss of baby flab.

'Your daughter is a runaway?' he said to her.

She paused. 'I – I hardly know how to answer,' she said, plucking at her skirt. She pressed on her fingernail so hard it broke.

The policeman from Radlett came and asked questions to which Rowena and Douglas could only provide answers that sounded, even to Rowena's ears, culpably vague. But to explain the nature of

Evangeline was difficult. Was she a backward child, he wanted to know? Was she handicapped? A candidate for electroshock treatment? Evangeline did not fit easily into any category, and yet she was considered mentally subnormal by those who saw her slipping, murmuring, sidling through the village in her ghost frocks. The villagers had plenty to say to the police about Miss Evangeline Crale. The station at Radlett brought in another officer from Watford. They rifled through Evangeline's trunk, contacted her old school in London, and interviewed all the neighbours. They spent the most time at Brinden, where the Pollards were apparently happy to answer questions and give them the run of the place, and they came back full of tales of Mrs Pollard's rock cakes and Mr Pollard's sloe gin.

'Have you seen her this week at *all*?' Rowena asked the twins, and dreaded the answer.

'No, Mummy,' said Rosemary.

Jennifer shook her head. 'No,' she said. There was something shuttered about her eyes.

The hay meadows were dozing, and the Dangerfields went to Cornwall, which meant that Rowena could wander freely. She resolved to keep Bob out in the sunshine and baby Caroline in the fresh air when she was not with Mrs Pollard. The village was a little emptier. She had hoped for a bucket-and-spade holiday perhaps in Essex or Suffolk, but Eva's absence rendered this an impossibility, while the expenses of the house prohibited it. 'Eva, Eva,' Rowena called, whenever no villager was near her. The police asked more questions and returned an officer to Brinden, but the frequency of Eva's past absences made them confident of an imminent return.

'There are wild children we occasionally come across, Mrs Crale,' said PC Baldihew from Radlett. 'They stray. They tend to return when the weather gets colder.'

'It's early August,' said Rowena, glancing at the glaring sky, the drying grass on the green. 'Are you saying she may return in *September*?'

'We would hope for an earlier return,' he said. 'And we will allocate it our full attention. But I am of the opinion that come the new school term and a chill in the air, your girl will come scurrying back like a rat.'

'Don't call my daughter a rat,' said Rowena. The green swayed a little. She felt woozy on the new pills, but she slept like the dead.

'We will be making further inquiries.'

'*Eva*,' Rowena called across the stream, as soon as the policeman had climbed on to his bicycle.

There was no echo, just a stillness, a trickle.

'She with Freddie,' said Bob.

Rowena stiffened.

'Is she?'

'Yus!' Bob nodded, grinned, and hopped about the flagpole socket in a circle.

'How do you know, darling?'

'I hear 'em.'

'Where?'

'There.'

'Where, Bobby?'

Bob pointed a fat finger towards their house, to the top windows.

'Upstairs?'

'Yus yus. Freddie down. *Down*stairs. Evie's friend. I sees 'im, hear 'im.'

'Me too,' murmured Rowena, and was frightened of herself, and shed a tear she wiped away with the back of her hand; then she took Bob paddling in the almost-dry stream, and they fed the ducks on the pond, and she bought him an ice cream at the post office shop.

'Sure your girl will come back,' said the owner comfortingly. 'Always did see her out dawn and dusk.'

There was a bending of the air, a coldness from the staircase, but no child there when she got back. Oh God, thought Rowena, catching sight of herself in a mirror and seeing how pale she was, how stringy and dulled the brightness of her auburn-brown hair.

Every day, the damp found a different course, bubbled in new patterns like fungus, emitted new smells, taunted her with fresh oozings, and the stairs and the landing were careless in their resentment, their aches and shadows and contractions of air. She kept herself outside, walking Bob about the village, wheeling Caroline after Mrs Pollard's, laying her on the grass. She sobbed every day, at odd times, for Evangeline, and walked further, out and about in the village, searching for her.

She asked Mrs Pollard if she could look round Brinden in case Eva was hiding there.

'Of course, my dear,' said Mrs Pollard, laying her hand sympathetically on her arm, and allowed her to search all over the house and land, where she tripped and crouched, torn between revulsion and fascination, and became as filthy as Evangeline.

Beyond a run of tool rooms, right at the back of the house, Rowena saw a door that had escaped her notice, a door almost obscured by the lack of light in that warren of neglected storage rooms, and she had to struggle past a tricycle and an old mangle to gain access. She turned the key that was left in the lock and pushed the door open with some difficulty. Inside was a room that was different from the others, and appeared to be half-finished. Its small window gave on to a bank of earth in that sunken back area of the house, a muddy slope that plunged it into semi-darkness. Rowena switched on the bulb overhead and saw a room in transition, seemingly half-prepared for a girl of uncertain age: in her early teens, or possibly much younger. Its floor was still covered in unvarnished boards with loose nails, the window as yet uncurtained, but its walls were papered pink, with a princess bed in one corner and a draped and sparkling dressing table in another.

It was apparent that this was nothing to do with Evangeline, who would have scorned such convention and left her own shabby mark. The sickly glycerine pink of the walls seemed to throb in the gloom, and among the froth of the dressing table sat a little Gaiety transistor, a *Gear Guide* and a copy of *June*, while a picture of a rag doll adorned one wall. A giant yellow teddy bear sat on the bed's pillow beside a Barbie with friend Midge.

'Who – what – *whose* is that room?' she asked Mrs Pollard.

'Which of the many, dear?' said Mrs Pollard without looking at her.

'The one at the back.'

Mrs Pollard's face was blank.

'Past the pantry by the back door, beyond all the tool storage shelves, the lawnmower . . .'

'Oh yes. For my niece,' she said in her smoothest cream voice.

'Oh,' said Rowena. She hesitated. 'What's her name?'

Mrs Pollard paused, barely perceptibly. 'Barbara,' she said.

By Thursday, Rowena was suddenly calmer, muffled by the dregs of dark deep sleep. Eva would come back – of course she would – Douglas always told her that, brusquely, though she noticed he was increasingly snappy on the subject.

'The child is not *right*,' he said to her in exasperation. 'You can't apply normal rules to her, Ro. She's – she's – she will be living off nuts and berries, jaunting around in her petticoats and sleeping in a bloody mob cap. The trouble she'll be in when she's back. I need to beat some sense into her.'

'No!' Rowena gasped. 'No, no, Douglas. You see. This is what I'm afraid of. When she comes back, we must *welcome* her.'

'You always were too soft on her, you know. The kid's touched, and that's that, I'm afraid.'

Rowena looked away from him and glanced out

of the window. Gregory Dangerfield was back that night from Cornwall.

The following morning, Rowena waited for Gregory to go to work, ventured on to the green and checked on Bob who was playing on the war memorial, then, desperate for distraction, she buried herself in the story of the extraordinary train robbery that had just occurred in Buckinghamshire. She watched the suntanned Dangerfield children, Peter and Jane, march to the post office, and then focused on Bob's head, in case Lana emerged. There was no sign of Eva. The mobile library turned up and stayed almost empty, its book covers glaring with sun. There was a shimmer in the elm leaves. That was all. Eva had often said that Freddie hid up in the trees. But the day was bright, and such distortions couldn't get her, she thought.

Back at the house, the stains, smell, dampness slammed into her with all the force they ever had, ganging up on her, taunting her. She leaned against a wall as a rush of nausea hit her, filling her mouth with saliva, and she ran to the lavatory. The sun blazed on to the ceiling and highlighted the mapping of madder stains, urine-dark streaks, bubbles and furry outcrops. She even thought she saw the shape of a small bristle of hair beneath the paintwork on the arch. She wanted to get out of this house, she thought, and deliberately thumped upstairs. A hush of voices stopped, a billow of air, a shuffle of footfall. Where? Where? It stank up there. She burst into Bob's room, into Eva and Caroline's, knocked on the walls everywhere, pushed them, looked up at the ceiling, and saw nothing, nothing but distortions of air and light. She heard them again. She smelled *Je Reviens*.

She glanced at her watch, the one Mrs Crale had given her, an elegant ladies' watch, more delicate and tasteful than anything else she owned. That woman had always outclassed her, and they both knew it. She sidled down her garden path keeping a lookout for Greg who would probably come home for lunch, and within a few minutes, there he was. She glanced back up at the house. She couldn't go in there without him.

'Greg!'

'Mrs Crale!'

'Greg. Please.'

'What is it, darling?'

'Please. Please. Come in. Please come upstairs. It's not right.'

'You're all flustered,' he said, putting his hand on her shoulder. 'Come along, Mrs Crale, this can't be so bad.'

'You mustn't call me that,' she said urgently. 'Please.'

'Why ever not? It's your name, isn't it? You shall be Lady Crale, then. The Honourable Rowena. "She walks in darkness, like the night."'

She turned to him. He lifted her hair from her forehead, and she shivered.

'What's not right, sweet Rowena?'

'The house. The noises. The leaks. The . . . oh, Greg, I hardly know how to say . . . This is Bob. Bob, this is our kind neighbour, come to help us look for – where the leak is. Can you play with your train?'

'Yus.'

'Good boy,' she said, and she handed him a biscuit in passing.

She pointed. The stairs were still now, merely a slight tensing of light visible on the upstairs landing. He strode up there and she followed, grateful.

Gregory walked slowly round the two bedrooms, the boxroom and bathroom on that side of the house. He looked up at the ceilings. Then, hoisting himself on to Eva's clothes trunk so Rowena winced, he stretched his head out of the window and elevated himself on to the frame to look along the roof.

'It's as I thought. There's a skylight there and a small amount of space that's not accounted for,' he said, brushing down his shirt and returning to the landing.

'Oh yes, it contains an old water tank,' said Rowena.

'Couldn't that be leaking?'

'Apparently it's all sealed off.'

'There are "noises"?'

'Oh,' she said. 'Yes. Noises. I can't really explain . . .'

'I can hear nothing.'

'No.'

The air was warm and still up there with Gregory beside her, blissfully peaceful. He kissed her, very quickly, on the lips. Freddie did not exist. Sunlight spread in tree-patterned undulations on the walls. Bob made choo-chooing sounds downstairs and a small trail of *Je Reviens* swam through the warmth.

'Hmmm,' said Gregory.

He started to press the walls, tapping and pulling at the tongue-and-groove Rowena had been so proud of when Pollard had installed it to cover unsightly bulges in the plaster and grace the corridor with a modern touch. He kept on, the scent of his warm skin and the faint perspiration of effort reaching Rowena as she leaned against the wall, in the sunshine, happy to be there, stilled, soothed, watching him. He went on for some time.

'See this,' he said, pointing to the beading where

the corridor turned a corner. 'There's something . . .
Here. See . . . I think this beading covers it. Yes. This
gives a little. Look, the end of the wood is placed
flush against the beading, but—' He pushed against
the tongue-and-groove, then pulled at it, and opened
a section that swung out like a stable door.

'My God,' murmured Rowena.

A choke of heated fetid air hit her with a *whump*.
She felt an instant punch of nausea, there in the hot
sunshine. The air was sour with old life, breath,
bedding; with traces of custard, Dettol, and an
undertow of *Je Reviens* that followed. Rowena gagged.
There was a suggestion of mutton fat, or tallow, of
old sealed-in human habitation. Dust poured in
agitated whirlpools, sucked on to the landing.

'My Lord,' said Gregory.

Rowena swayed a little.

'Are you all right, darling?' he said.

She hung her head. She shook it.

'I'll fetch you water. Hold on, Rowena.'

The smell settled, then rose again, and she sank
carefully to her knees. She sat very still and let herself
open her eyes.

From the floor, she could see a section of a small
shelf that she recognised as having belonged in Mrs
Crale's room, with a bevelled mirror on top. And there
in the dust and sun dazzle was her mother-in-law,

looking startled, terrified, an emaciated face with shocked milky eyes and mouth in a mirror.

But there wasn't. Quite clearly there wasn't. It was the light over the dirty surface of the glass, and the smell, thickened by the heat, which immediately brought back in intensified form the presence of the old Evangeline Crale.

'Oh, Greg,' she moaned, a thin stream of saliva filling her mouth.

'What is it?' he said, taking the stairs two at a time with a glass of water. 'Drink this.' He crouched down beside her and held her shoulders.

'I am going mad.'

'No, you're not, darling.'

'Oh, Greg. I don't know . . .'

'Let me go in there.'

He helped her to her feet, then he ducked and disappeared under the section of wall above the tongue-and-groove panelling. 'Come in. Careful of your head,' he said.

Still shaking, warding away the sick image of Mrs Crale's face, she followed him. There behind the wall was a miniature Victorian room.

She gaped. Sun poured in a vigorous beam from the skylight, a bar of dust at her feet, the corners in shadow. She felt momentarily dizzy.

'My word,' he said. 'I can't believe this. What is it?'

She shook her head, her face close to his. There was barely space for both of them. The excess of dust, the rank heated air, made it hard to breathe.

'It must have been an airing cupboard once,' he said. 'Look, there's the sealed-off plumbing for a tank. But by Jove—'

Three slatted shelves ran alongside one wall of a room barely bigger than a large cupboard. The lower two shelves appeared to have functioned as small bunks, padded with lumpy layer upon layer of old linen, eiderdown, yellowing lace pillow, patchwork, dimity, bolster. The top shelf housed a battered jigsaw of crammed-in possessions. This airless tribute to a past era was lined with a faded floral wallpaper almost obscured by sconces, samplers, watercolours, framed miniatures, the floor carpeted with a chrysanthemum-splashed oriental rug, worn through at its middle.

'My God, I'm a little faint,' said Rowena.

'I'm not surprised, darling,' he said, holding her. 'This is . . . this is a time warp.'

'This must – this must —' she said, but she was too queasy to talk. She swallowed. 'This must have been my mother-in-law's,' she said eventually.

'What did she *do* here? Immure herself? Hide priests? Refugees?'

Rowena shook her head, barely able to talk.

A stiff buttoned chair with clawed feet stood in a corner, piled to its antimacassar with dust-strewn tins that Rowena recognised with a shudder of recognition advertised Mrs Crale's favourite foods – Jacob's crackers, custard powder, fish paste, New Berry Fruits and shortbread. Lace, crewelwork, jewellery, candlesticks and ornaments filled all surfaces, a row of china-faced Victorian dolls lining one shelf, a pair of porcelain dogs guarding the door. There was barely room to stand. The glass in the skylight showed a mess of old fingerprints in the dust. Brass light fittings were attached to wall and sloping ceiling; a clutter of ammonites, ink wells, dust-draped dried flowers laced with cobweb were piled on a washstand. Books were stacked in rows at the bottom of each bunk. A stained chamber pot Rowena didn't want to look at closely lay under the piled-up lower bunk. The dust and close air made her want to retch. She did. 'Sorry,' she murmured.

'I have never seen anything like it,' said Greg slowly. 'What is this? A crazy antique shop?'

Rowena started. In a corner behind the one small chair sat a bird in a domed glass display cabinet. She stared through the bar of illuminated dust into the shadows. It was the same type of bird as the pet of Mrs Crale's that had recently died, a canary, but it was badly stuffed so its poor body was lumpy and listing, its eyes non-existent. There was an area of condensation on the inside of the glass. Rowena let out a small murmur as she caught the dead-bird smell that had met the damp in the sitting room after the wall had fallen, but she knew it was in her imagination, and she looked up at Gregory, willing him to take charge.

'It is remarkable. The secrets you keep, Mrs— Lady Crale.'

'Greg, please,' said Rowena, taking in a big breath. 'Please let's not tell Douglas. It will upset him. His mother seemed a bit . . . strange . . . increasingly as the years have gone on, when she still lived here, and this is very disturbing.'

'Disgusting, really.'

'Yes, *disgusting*.'

'Let's just shut it back up,' said Gregory in the gung-ho manner Rowena found so appealing.

'Yes. Yes, please do. He'll start banging around it, accusing Pollard of being incompetent, getting the new builders to investigate. I think he'll find it terribly upsetting, evidence of her . . . mental disturbance. Obviously the leak's not coming from there.'

She found she was speaking fast, trying to keep away the agitation, the thought of Mrs Crale's face.

'No, there is no radiator or tap in there. It's like

a doll's house. Meets an old people's home. It's Miss Havisham. It's—'

'Less romantic. It stinks,' said Rowena with a shudder.

They went back downstairs and stood in the sitting room. Behind her back, the shadows gathered, and the water on the quarry tiles glinted in the light. Bob was playing with it, staining his shirt grey, and she snatched him up. She knew the other boy would tug at her mind once Greg had left, would be there with his needs and love.

She was being persecuted, Rowena thought, and a wave of indignation hit her. The room above would be rank in the sunshine, abandoned as it had been for how much time? With the amount of dust in there, it could have been years. It was evidence of madness, she mused. The old lady had become loopy. *Evangeline*, she thought. Poor touched Evangeline. How much madness was there in the family, then? Douglas was so sensible. But an old lady who could have hidden herself in a cupboard, recreating her childhood in dotage, was clearly unwell. Rowena felt a new sense of righteousness that soothed the guilt, yet had a simultaneous premonition that it would jump out at her once more, and catch her round the throat.

'Oh God. I want to get away from here,' she

murmured, and looked at Gregory, who was frowning up at the ceiling with its stains. He was beautiful, daring, heedless, she thought, and she needed him to rescue her from the damp and the shadows and the half-sensed boy, the lost girl, and this house and herself. Through the despair, a shiver of desire took her. It was sunny outside. The sky was a raging blue.

'I need to get out.'

He glanced at his watch. 'Come to the power station with me.' He held her tighter.

She gazed at him.

'Come on, poor Bob's barking in the car. He's probably roasted.'

'The dog's called Bob?'

'Like your son. Come on. Where will you leave boy Bob?'

'I can't leave him!'

A momentary expression of impatience crossed his face. 'My secretary will look after him. She will be very suspicious. Good. He can play with the dog. Bob and Bob bobbing.'

'You're so silly!'

'Come along.' He twined his fingers with hers, pressed his lips to her knuckles.

'Let's make a run for it. I'm parked near the hedge. If anyone sees us, I'm giving you a lift to Elstree.'

Outside, the dancing roar of sunshine hit them;

she was dizzy and she laughed as he hoisted Bob and helped Rowena into the car.

'Bump bump bump,' said Bob, running his hand over Bob the dog's back.

'Yes, we think it's something at the station giving him lumps,' said Gregory cheerfully. 'He runs like a lunatic round the fields all day, slurps God knows what in the water, then comes back and hits the floor like a corpse.'

Rowena turned her head back, almost as a ritual, a talisman, and looked at the house. The sun glanced off the skylight. She was relieved to be leaving it.

'He'll probably turn green,' said Gregory, and revved the car and span along the horse-chestnut-arched road out of the village. '*One* day,' he said, 'she will be replaced by an E-Type Roadster. And we will dine together at the Dorchester, then park where no one can see.'

12

At the power station, Gregory handed his jacket to his secretary and issued some instructions, taking a call in impatient tones before he sat down. Rowena watched him through the window of his office as he swung on his chair behind an oversized desk and poured himself a drink. She sat outside, pretending to read a magazine. Once, just once, he turned in her direction as he spoke on the phone and looked directly at her, his eyes holding promise, rebellion, intent.

She smiled at him, and at herself behind her magazine, and she felt refreshingly elegant there in that place of glaring secretaries in dated spectacles and engineers in masks and white suits. She wandered to the door, hoping Greg was watching her. Bob was playing in the fields with Bob, throwing a stick mere inches and stumbling, grinning.

'Lady Crale, allow me to show you round my power station,' said Gregory Dangerfield, his breath a sudden heat on her temple, and they wandered round rooms of steel to the sounds of humming and pumping, past the generator and turbine areas, straight past signs that said *Danger*.

He kissed her suddenly. My daughter's whereabouts are uncertain, she thought. My husband is not desirable to me. My house is putrefying around me. She needed, very urgently, to block it out. He was kissing her neck, kissing her collarbone. He put his hand under the strap of her dress, and she gazed at him, limp with desire, knees barely able to prop her up, but there were footsteps nearby and they fell apart.

'Come here,' he said, and pulled her into an office, but there were too many workers around, and too much glass.

'I want to make love to you. Very badly,' he murmured.

They went past the control room to a small concrete area behind, and they kissed against a wall, near dark puddles that reminded her, though she fought the image, of the tiles in her house. She saw the carved glory of his mouth and he told her she

was the most beautiful creature, a breathing manne-
quin, a woman of dreams, that he was falling for
her, and then a receptionist tapped past on high
heels and they slipped behind a frozen tank, and
waited.

'We need to find somewhere,' said Greg. 'I will
find somewhere.'

Rosemary, Jennifer and baby Caroline were at
Brinden. 'Rosemary dear,' said Mrs Pollard. 'Fetch
me my sunshade, will you? Mr Pollard is off working
in Watford today.'

Rosemary nodded and set off on her peg legs to
fetch a parasol from the hall. She was wearing a pale
yellow shorts-and-bib playsuit that did not flatter
her.

The babies dozed, fast asleep in the heat.

'Jennifer, you need your orange juice, dear,' said
Mrs Pollard, picking up the cap she was crocheting
for her, and putting it down. 'Not in this heat,' she
murmured. 'And one more brush of your hair. I
bought you – Jennifer, when I was at my sister's
house in Bushey, I bought you a Sindy doll book
to cut out and dress. I only bought Rosemary some
sweet cigarettes. Do you think they will be enough?'
she said anxiously. 'I have bought poor Evangeline
nothing, of course.'

'Thank you, Mrs Pollard,' said Jennifer politely. Her hair danced and dazzled in the glare.

Rosemary returned and sucked on her sweet cigarettes, two at a time. She stuck one behind her ear. Jennifer giggled.

'Jennifer, my dear, now you can sit here and talk nicely to me whilst I try to set those curls in this dreadful heat,' said Mrs Pollard. 'Mr Pollard will sketch you as a country maiden, holding some of his flowers, when he gets back later.' She turned to the drying fields. 'I see no sign of a girl in a pale frock and petticoats today,' she mused.

'No, Mrs Pollard,' said Jennifer.

'Look! He's not in Watford,' said Rosemary as Pollard appeared with his clipboard and paper. 'He's not,' she said, pointing at the shelter. 'He's there.'

'So he is,' said Mrs Pollard placidly.

'I want to go home now,' said Jennifer.

'Not yet, dear,' said Mrs Pollard.

Jennifer was silent for a few minutes.

'But Mummy asked us to hang up the washing so it dries before evening,' she said uncertainly.

'Time for your orange juice, dear,' said Mrs Pollard in her custard cream voice.

'We have to look more urgently for Eva,' said Rowena as soon as Douglas came home that night.

'Yes,' he said. 'Police round here are as ineffectual as the builders. Not that this new lot have cured these blasted problems either.'

In the night, there was old Mrs Crale, both half-demented child and crone, with her bedpan and her doll's-house room. She came trailing that eternal foul guilt. In the daytime, Rowena could periodically muffle the guilt, sidestep it, or even accept its validity, head bowed; but at night it was a monster that fed on her. It was Mrs Crale's face, the expression on it when she and Douglas had told her that she wasn't coping and that they had been in contact with her goddaughter, that was preserved in her mind and which always toppled her, the absolute panic in her poor faded eyes. The protest, agitation, weak attempts to prove her independence. Rowena turned away to face her pillow, Douglas snuffling beside her. Gregory Dangerfield came to her, and now in the depths of the night, her desire froze into pure panic. She turned abruptly to the ceiling, and Mrs Crale returned. There was no escape.

Rowena tensed her legs, threw her sheet back, utterly restless, and then she thought she heard a noise. It was from the other side of the house. She listened. Her bedroom was in the back section, the former number 2, facing Gregory's lawn, merci-fully far from that landing and staircase in the old number 3, and everything in her resisted walking through those passages in the dark, but she needed to check on Bob and Caroline. The bulb outside her bedroom had blown. She crept along, the wall-paper with its racing-boat design leading her to the doorway, the step and staggered landing before the former number 3, and there she paused. She listened, her heart thumping. There was nothing, she reassured herself. She could hear her own breathing. Then there was a shuffling sound, like a light footfall, a rodent.

Could *Eva* have returned, and discovered that stuffed cupboard? They were so close, those two: had old Mrs Crale revealed to her this fusty doll's room on some visit in the past, before they had moved in? Did Eva now hide there as well as wherever else it was she stayed? Yet with its dust and stale closed air, it clearly hadn't been entered for some time.

'Eva,' she said, unsteadily, and knocked lightly. 'Eva,' she murmured, hoping against sense. She pressed her ear to the wood, straining to hear more. There was a general rustling, a flurry of floorboards shifting, pipes contracting, her own heartbeat hammering over the top. But wasn't this always the way? If you listened for long enough at night in an old house on the edge of a village, weren't there settlings and expansions, weather movements, animal sounds? Yet there were voices, quiet voices, she was certain of it: a hushed, murmuring layering of sounds. Were they coming from the pub outside? She ran into Caroline and Eva's bedroom, creeping past the cot, and listened from under the window. The sounds from outside – a car door, a couple of drunken calls – were quite distinct.

She went back on to the landing. There were pattering footsteps, the inching of a door. Her heart daggered into her throat. She couldn't move. Someone tapped her leg and she yelped.

'Mummy!'

She jumped. 'Bobby! Oh God, Bob.' She picked him up with a rough movement. He wriggled. 'Bob,' she said, her heart banging against him. 'My Bobbit. Why are you awake?'

'They're here,' he said.

She swallowed. She tried to catch her breath. 'Who? Where are "they"?'

He clambered back down, smiled, shrugged, pointed at the wall, then further down the passage, back at his room, and span round, grinning, pointing in all directions.

'Yes, darling, and what do you hear?'

'Dem peoples. Cats. Lady crying!'

'Crying? How?'

He shrugged again. 'Freddie here? But Eva not lookin' after now? Poor Freddie.'

'Bob, darling,' said Rowena, pulling his head to her and stroking it rhythmically. 'Tell me more. Have you *seen* any of these people, cats, Freddie?'

He hesitated. 'No,' he said, looking up at her, eyes big dark pools in the night. 'Yes,' he said.

'OK, darling,' said Rowena, with a forced calm. 'Tell me what they look like.'

He shook his head.

'No? Nothing?'

'Freddie is Freddie!' He giggled.

'What about the other ones?'

'No,' he said, his expression suddenly stiff.

'Please, Bob. What do the others look like?'

He shook his head, tugging at her hand.

'Please tell me.'

He shook his head. A tear wobbled from his eye, fear tangible on his face.

'Bob—'

He began to cry, snuffling tears as he buried his face in her legs.

'Shh, hush,' she said, holding him to her. 'Don't wake the baby.'

She put him back to bed, and stroked him till he was sleeping, then tiptoed out.

She steeled herself. Almost calling aloud in her

fear, she pressed at the panel of tongue-and-groove, running her fingers down the edge of the beading. As Gregory had said, it was flush against the planks; there was nothing visible. She put her hands exactly where she thought she remembered him pressing, but she could feel no movement under her fingers, as though the wood met solid wall. She pressed further down, but nothing gave. She was largely relieved. The night was silent, and finally she crept back into the other side of the house and into her bed.

13

The next morning, the stains on the ceiling above the arch formed a crazy network, a scrabble of angles that resembled beaks, feet, trampled feathers. A section of plaster was working loose, a brown-edged rough-toothed shard of it. There was that smell of urine again, thought Rowena, that sourness they had unearthed when they attacked the wall: cat's piss, something rank and wet like damp straw. The *Je Reviens* was the tiniest note behind it. She remembered Mrs Crale wetting herself, and shuddered. She *had* needed care, she thought, trying to comfort herself. But it had not been a pure decision. She now cursed the day she had thought of moving here: it had been her idea, not Douglas's, though he had edged towards it with a series of doubts that had turned into justifications. She cursed the day. What was hers was not hers.

The phone rang. It was PC Baldihew calling in somewhat weary tones from Radlett. The police were clearly losing interest in their search as there were reports of sightings of this wild girl who was, to their eyes, little but a troubled runaway.

'We *have* to find her,' said Rowena. 'This isn't her . . . normal pattern of disappearances. Is it? Douglas?'

'No,' grunted Douglas.

A shadow of a child passed the doorway in the next room. Rowena looked up. 'Have we got——?'

She was silent.

'Have we got what?' said Douglas absently as he looked through the London telephone directory.

'Was there someone in there?'

'No.'

'I – where's Bob?'

'In the khazi last time I looked. I need to go . . . Can you get my newer shirts ironed today? And weren't we meant to invite the Dangerfields for dinner? Have them round with the Bradshaws?'

'Yes,' said Rowena quietly.

She looked down at her pinny after he had left to meet the cricket team for a Saturday lunch in the pub. She was crumpled, not yet model-trim, and she was to spend her day in a round of domestic tasks that after all these years as a housewife still felt somewhat beyond her capabilities. Her mother hadn't taught her adequately, as Douglas had hinted over the years. She wondered what had happened to that grammar school girl who, the teachers had all agreed, should go to university. The girl who had taken a secretarial course instead because her parents had thought it more useful, and then met Douglas Crale. What had happened to the girl who read reams of Wordsworth, Racine, Chaucer? Who knew the order of the kings and queens of England and could recite the periodic table of the elements? She missed that earnest prize-winner in a blue blouse who had not yet discovered that certain men found her attractive, that there was fun to be had in clubs and coffee bars. And five children? *Five?* She could never, ever have imagined as she sat there with her Latin primer that her body would bear her so many children.

'I've seen Eva,' said Jennifer.

'What? *Where?*'

Jennifer hesitated for the tiniest fraction of a second. 'Mrs Pollard's.'

'Have you seen her, Rosemary?' said Rowena rapidly.

Rosemary turned to her mother slowly, then shook her head.

Rowena looked at Jennifer. 'You haven't seen her, have you?' she snapped, instinct informing her.

Jennifer widened her eyes until they were oversized blue jewels. They are utterly utterly blank, thought Rowena with a quiver of distaste. I don't trust her. She is hiding something.

'Douglas,' said Rowena in desperation after her husband had made a noisy return home already tipsy and she had poured him a drink. 'There's something I should – show you. In case, in case, Eva—' She held him protectively. 'Please don't be upset—'

She left him upstairs and wandered out to the garden to avoid the sounds of him thundering about and cursing. His anger had always turned her rigid.

'A sighting!' said Gregory through the laurel.

Rowena jumped.

'I am in luck,' he said.

She cast her gaze quickly about her.

'You've been waiting,' she said boldly.

'Right first time. Come to a hotel with me?'

Electricity swarmed up her body. She looked at her feet. 'You know I can't do that,' she said.

'Where? Where then, heavenly creature? You know I want to *be* with you so badly.'

'Hush,' said Rowena in a low voice, but all she

wanted to do was slash her way through the hedge and place herself in his arms.

'Stay home from church? Tomorrow?'

She dropped her gaze again. She paused. 'I'll try.' She coloured. She turned her head. 'Douglas,' she hissed, ran her hand through her hair and returned, aware of Gregory's gaze on her back. Her steps were unsteady.

Evangeline hovered over her as she did every time such desire caught her, and Mrs Crale appeared ghost-like behind her, prodding her with guilt and now outrage. Then the lust took over again. It was urgent. It blocked out the rest, for moments, like some divine drug tumbling through her body, and left a later residue of even more bitter guilt.

Douglas, white-faced, crashed down the stairs. Rowena tried to hold him, but he was stiff, and she fetched him another drink. He swayed slightly. She could smell the alcohol on him and see the beads of cooling sweat on his forehead.

'It's *obscene*,' he said. 'Like a cluttered — coffin.'

'I know, darling, I know.'

'Revolting. Poor Mother. Oh Jesus, Ro.'

'Darling, I'm sorry.'

'Yes, well. Poor old— But Eva? Ro, it's covered in dust and cobwebs. No one's been there for months, years. Let's shut it up and forget it.'

'Yes, darling. I think so too.'

'Later we could get it cleared and use it for suit-cases or the like,' he said, sweeping his fingers wildly through his hair. 'But I'm going to get the rest of the bloody house done first. The infernal damp.'

'I agree,' she said.

That night they tried to make love without success, but she felt relief that she had done her duty for a while in at least attempting it.

In the early hours of the morning, Rowena woke up, restless. She was overheated, her nightdress sticking to her as fantasy after fantasy about Gregory Dangerfield ballooned through the summer stillness. She seemed to pour her desire like a thick black rope through her window and through the night garden to where he lay sleeping less than a hundred yards away. One moment she thought she could meet him the following morning; the next, she was shocked at her own foolhardiness.

She thought about Lady Chatterley's Mellors in the garden, trying to recall every scene she had read. As she lay there kissing Gregory, she heard footsteps. They were not like the rustling and murmuring layers of sound she thought she heard near Bob's room. Distinctly, she heard footsteps. She rose and glided across the room in her pale blue lawn nightdress, and

Gregory was watching her, pulling back her hair in one hard cool movement and taking her to him to kiss her; then she opened her bedroom door, and there was Jennifer in her clothes, descending the stairs.

Rowena followed her out of the house, and into the garden.

'Jennifer!'

Rowena yanked her shoulder as she started along the garden path.

Jennifer turned to her quite calmly. 'I couldn't sleep,' she said.

'What are you doing?'

'I was taking some air.'

Rowena frowned at her: even the phrase was not her own.

'Were you going to go out of the gate?'

Jennifer hesitated. 'No, Mummy,' she said.

'I think you've started lying to me,' said Rowena, suddenly uncharacteristically angry. She took both Jennifer's shoulders and shook her slightly. 'Haven't you?'

Jennifer widened her eyes.

'No, Mummy.'

'You are just thirteen. It is not safe at night out there. There are sometimes gypsies about, foxes . . . That strange sect nearby with all the long-haired people . . .'

Jennifer smiled. 'I'll go back to bed.'

Rowena caught her hands. 'Where is Eva?' she said.

Jennifer gazed up at her. In the light of the moon meeting the street lamp, she looked like a film star, illuminated by a glow as she had so singularly not been on screen. She wrinkled her brow. 'I don't know,' she said.

As the birds began their chaotic chorus, Rowena finally slept.

'The children need their breakfast,' said Douglas, shaking her awake two hours later, and she groaned and staggered downstairs in a daze of head pain and fatigue. Dully, she cooked Ready Brek on the new hob.

'You look peaky,' said Douglas. 'Wretched.'

'I feel wretched,' she murmured.

'Church in an hour,' he said. 'People don't miss it here.'

'I . . .' she said. 'I need to get some sleep.'

'I woke Mummy in the night,' said Jennifer suddenly.

Douglas nodded. He looked round, then clapped his hands. 'Come on, kids. Get to your posts. We're going to church on our own. Chop chop.'

✳

Rowena spotted him from the bedroom at the end of his garden as she had in the tumble of her fantasies, though in the night he had been in a white shirt as though dressed for work. She raced to the bath, visibly shaking under the shallow water, pulled in her stomach, re-shaved her legs and cut herself, wincing as she applied antiperspirant; she dressed in her new pedal pushers, knotted a shirt at her waist, and inspected her face, hiding from her window and slapping a little colour into her cheeks. Freckles danced across her nose over a tan from her perambulations about the green in his absence, rendering her instantly more youthful after so much time in which she had felt merely hag-ridden. She decided to keep her hair loose beneath a wide band so it fell with a bounce at either side of her face. She glanced out of the window again, glimpsed patches of white moving behind the foliage, and emerged on the garden path. She heard a low whistle. She walked slowly to the laurel.

'I am flying, allegedly,' Gregory Dangerfield said, his eyes catching hers through the leaf-shade. 'But I fear the plane will have developed a fault. And you are . . . ?'

'Sleeping,' said Rowena, blushing.

He was wearing a T-shirt, like Marlon Brando, and the contours of his chest were visible as never before beneath the cotton, the muscles on his arms almost, she thought, like sexual organs — too frank, too male. Her mouth was slack. She was aware she must look half-witted.

'Come round the front,' he said. 'They're all at church. Hasten, Lady Crale.'

'You know I mustn't, I mustn't . . .' she said, trailing off.

'Do you wish to talk, walk, drink elderflower cordial?' he said and took her by the waist, his hand a light pressure on its curve, and automatically the desire for him to want her grew, the longing for him blotting her vision.

She hesitated. He smiled, reading her.

'Come and see the children's tree house,' he said, almost laughing, and her heart accelerated alarmingly, weakening her legs as she climbed the small ladder to the tree house that sat brightly in a cage of oak. She crouched down to enter it. It was uncharming, paint-new, and appeared almost unused by those spoilt children with their own swings and bars, their many pets and Wendy house. The church spire was visible, roofs, hedges and fences. Motor cars in many colours were converging by the green for a rally that was being held that day.

'Do sit, Lady Crale,' he said, and they lowered themselves and sat in a tangle of limbs on the floor with its rug and cushions, their legs almost reaching the other end.

There was a hooting on the green as the car rally gathered momentum. 'Ignore them,' he said, and he flipped her on to her back, skilfully in that small space. 'Ingenuity is required,' he said as he unhooked her bra, that beautiful gingham patterned object she treasured, that she could wear now she was no longer required as a dairy cow, and he was above her, the oak leaves patterning the corners of her vision as she pulled him to her, their legs at odd angles and their clothes tangled ridges as they laughed at themselves. She kissed him rapidly all over his cheeks, chin, mouth: fast kisses everywhere, until he shifted his position and stilled her, slowed her, kissed her with great tenderness. He faced her, his hair falling forward, his expression intent and focused and almost brutal as she had never seen it before, so she momentarily wanted to escape, but he whispered to her and she needed him, so needed him, and he was above her and inside her and she shuddered as cars hooted and voices began sounding from the green as the congregation left the church.

14

'Where is Jennifer?' said Rowena when Douglas returned.

She had changed into her weekend drainpipes and a checked shirt; she was sore, her thighs tender and her head light, almost stupefied in her distraction. The clamour of motors and voices above them bounced in through the windows in a constant stream as though a wireless were on.

'She must be behind us,' said Douglas. He was not cross and overheated as she had expected, but pleased with himself, calling Bob 'old man' and praising the behaviour of the girls. He even ruffled Caroline's downy hair, making her cry.

'Good, good,' said Rowena, smiling. '*Lunch!*' she

said suddenly. She had not given it a moment's consideration.

'I thought, I thought—' she said hastily. 'We would have a summer salad.' She snatched eggs in a dangerous fashion from the fridge and put a pan on to boil. 'I have been asleep, not much time . . . beetroot salad, egg, lettuce . . .' she said, hiding behind the fridge door.

Douglas darkened. 'I'm peckish,' he said. 'When will we eat?'

'Soon,' said Rowena, searching for crackers as the bread was stale. Cars were revving and hooting. 'And . . . sausages,' she said brightly.

'Dreadful racket. How *long* did you sleep?'

'Oh, ages,' said Rowena. 'Silly me. When Jennifer woke me in the night, I couldn't . . . Where *is* she, Douglas?'

'Where's Jennifer?' he said to Rosemary, not turning.

'I don't know,' said Rosemary. 'Shall I go and look, Daddy?'

'Yes. She's probably being chatted to by the vicar's wife,' he said. 'You know how a certain kind of silly woman seems to dote on Jennifer.'

'It's the ones without their own children,' murmured Rowena, scooping mayonnaise in a daze. She boiled eggs and laid the table, waiting for Rosemary and Jennifer to return.

Rosemary ran in, out of breath. 'She's not there,' she said.

'Who is still at the church?' said Rowena.

'No one now,' said Rosemary.

'Oh,' said Rowena. Faint anxiety started fanning through her distraction.

'No one?' said Douglas.

'They've closed the church now. The vicar is gone, Daddy. The people were all watching the motor cars.'

'Some terrific marques,' he said. 'Well, she must be amongst them.'

'I didn't see her, Daddy,' said Rosemary.

'She didn't go home with a friend?' said Rowena.

Rosemary shook her head. 'She wouldn't on a Sunday lunchtime without asking you. Would she?'

'I'll pop out and have a look for her. But oh, lunch.'

'Honestly,' said Douglas, opening a beer and running his hand through his hair. 'Can't it wait? I'm famished.'

Rowena ate virtually nothing. The beetroot was watery, the cubed cheese hard, the lettuce sparse. Douglas was openly disgruntled, but she barely responded. Her breasts had been touched. Her nipples were hard at the memory. She swayed very slightly.

'I am going to find Jennifer,' she said, standing up.

'I think I'll go to the pub for a ploughman's,' said Douglas in a tight voice.

'Look after the babies,' Rowena said to Rosemary, and ran out to the green, where she cast her eyes around for Evangeline even as she looked for Jennifer, and Freddie seemed to follow her out there too. He was clinging to her skirt; she felt it, a child in the bright sunshine tugging at her impatiently, but then he was gone, his presence only a shadow by the stream, if at all, and the green rippled in a heat haze, and she was furious with herself for such arrant stupidity.

The rally was now thinning, and Lally Lyn, who was signing an autograph through a car window, waved.

'Have you seen Jennifer?' Rowena called, but Lally was still chatting to her fan. She stood in the girlish knock-kneed pose she used in photographs. 'Sorry, duck,' she mouthed, then made her way in a swirling blouse that looked to Rowena like the Pucci she saw in magazines, and was approached by another driver.

Rowena clicked her tongue in impatience. 'Please,' she asked anyone she saw, 'have you seen Jennifer?'

She knocked on a few doors. She tried houses

where the twins knew the children. A cloud of panic was rising inside her.

'Lost another bairn?' said the small Scottish man who lived in a tiny house divided into two behind the pub.

Rowena gasped. She lifted her hand, and without hesitation she slapped his face. Then she gaped at him.

'Sorry,' she said, widening her eyes. 'I'm most awfully sorry.'

He stared at her, his mouth tightening.

She backed off, apologising, and ran around the village. Eventually, she made herself approach the Dangerfield house. She stood on the step, quite dizzy with dread. As she lifted her hand to the polished brass knocker, she had to steady her breathing.

There they all were, at lunch in their large dining room, the remains of a Sunday roast on the table as they tucked into a trifle. Gregory visibly tensed as he saw her. Her hair was ragged; she was perspiring; her casual outfit was infinitely less appealing than the clothes she had worn when he had made love to her. Lana Dangerfield was somewhat reserved.

'I've not seen her,' she said in her careful tones. 'I'm sorry.'

Peter and Jane gazed silently.

*

The police searched everywhere that day, bringing in a larger force and scouring and interviewing the village. Locals joined them in the evening, searching the outlying fields and woods. The reaction to the disappearance of Jennifer was in sharp contrast to that of Eva, who was clearly considered a lost cause and prone to wandering. The police announced that by the following day, they would release the news to the public.

'If this pack of rural bobbies doesn't find her,' said Douglas, 'I'm thinking we need to hire a private detective. Get a proper chap up here. It will cost us, Ro.'

'They're already bringing in a bigger force,' she said. 'But yes. Yes. Please let's do that.'

'If you get the press on to it, lie low, darling,' Gregory murmured to Rowena over her garden gate. 'You'll have to gag Lally Lyn, otherwise she'll be offering up quotes about how "fabsville" it was playing Jennifer's sister to the *Herald*. I'll have a word with her,' he said, swinging his work jacket on to his shoulder. 'You don't want the press getting hold of the – two . . .'

Rowena sobbed and put her face in her hands.

'Hold tight,' he said and gazed momentarily into her eyes. He squeezed her hand. 'I'll see you as soon as I can.'

*

In the night, there was no sleep. Image upon image processed past her: her children were taken from her by the court, the adoption services, inevitable if you *lost* two of five, three of six, the sums merging in her head so she was sweating and crying and begging her pillow. *Jennifer, Jennifer*, she sobbed. While Eva had always wandered, especially now they lived in the country, Jennifer trod a safe path between home, village and friends' houses, with occasional excursions across the fields to Brinden with her sisters. Douglas woke intermittently and threw his arm around Rowena, or sighed heavily at her sleeplessness; once he paced the floor and left the room and she heard the sounds of him muttering Jennifer's name as he urinated loudly. He crashed back to sleep, and she rose to go to the bathroom herself and heard the noises so openly now, the creaks and murmurings from along the passage. She almost didn't care.

She walked through the house in her nightdress, and the sounds subsided but the smells were there in force, the landing thick with perfume, with – she had to face it – with urine, and, as she descended the staircase at that end, the air was hung with mildew, with sour wafts of cat. Was there canary there too? No, that was in her imagination. She gagged. The stains were now spreading from above the arch to the middle of the ceiling, a crazy feathering of yellow, brown, rust on the paint, mould fingering towards the centre, its path interrupted by loosening sections of plaster, and spreading into plump furry accretions that recalled again Mrs Crale's old wallpaper, the birds that were decapitated by Pollard's blows. 'Oh God,' murmured Rowena. 'God,' she said more loudly, crying in some way for help.

'I seen your bairn,' said the old Scottish man the next day.

'Where?' Rowena gripped him.

'By the stream.'

'By the stream?' said Rowena rapidly. 'What was she *doing*?'

'Chatterin' away. As to a wee bairn. But there were none there.'

'Oh, you mean *Eva*?'

He looked puzzled. 'The lassie who dresses as the dead. As the departed. Like her grandmammy. As the—'

'Evangeline,' snapped Rowena, the neighbour's small wizened face with its hen eyes boring into her, and she felt that same impulse to hit him. 'You saw her?'

'Aye.'

'Where did she go afterwards?'

'I dinnae know.'

Rowena swore under her breath. 'Well, tell the police you saw her.'

'Aye. I will do that.'

'And if you see her again, *tell her to come home,* then fetch me. Tell her she won't be in trouble.'

'She will though, aye? Your mister will take a belt to her.'

Rowena went back to the house, sobbing. Douglas was betraying a new tone of urgency in his somewhat aggressive dealings with the police and she wanted to be near the phone. She gazed, all afternoon, out of the window, keeping Rosemary, Bob and Caroline inside, close to her. She had been prescribed a stronger dose of Librium. The light was mobile in the next room.

Freddie. Freddie is here, she thought – Freddie, who doesn't exist. My own girls are gone, *gone,* and all I have is a lost boy.

Eventually, Caroline and Bob went for their naps, Rosemary sat in her bedroom, and Rowena stood alone by the window. She gazed and gazed through different panes, the distortions of each small section of glass altering the view of the green in cloud, in rain, in silver silence, and she was increasingly aware that, should she look round, there would be someone behind her. She didn't look, but there was the knowledge of being watched, of someone small playing, the smell of grubby, sugary skin pressed against her back, and she stood there rigidly, the only movement the tears running down her face.

15

Rowena continued to look through the rain as the boy played behind her, a presence as sure as the clouds that darkened the room, while the faintest shiftings of joists sounded upstairs. She couldn't look at him or he would scutter away, a collection of shadows, so she resisted him with her back, and tears made her face sore as rain twined down the window.

Was she to call him Freddie? He had never had a name. 'Freddie,' she murmured aloud, to try it out, and she was reminded of Eva again, as she followed him up the stairs, because he was pulling at her with a hot sticky hand, and she would look after him now, when it was too late. Too late. He needed a mother's arms.

On the landing, he was gone, but there was Eva's skirt.

'Oh!' Rowena let out a cry.

A layer of red flannel petticoat beneath a sprigged flounce caught in the corner of the tongue-and-groove door; a hand opened the section again swiftly and quietly and then released it, and the wall was once again as it ever had been.

Joy flooded through Rowena. *Here* was her darling daughter. She cried thanks to God in the sky, in the clouds and heavens. If Evangeline was here, Jennifer was somewhere at large too. She was, she was; she had to be.

Rowena heard Eva's voice and caught her breath. Her heart was thumping so hard, she thought that surely its reverberations must drum on the wood, but she made herself still in her light-headedness, and she listened.

She heard murmurings, seemingly a conversation rising and falling through the noise of rain on the roof, and strained to hear the words. Eva! Her dear mad daughter, there in that horrible cupboard. Through her bewilderment was the blessed relief that the panic was over.

'. . . please,' said Eva gently.

There were whisperings, silences, a tangle of words. Rain thundered, subsided, regathered force, blocking out all other sound. Rowena pressed her ear harder to the wood, but she could distinguish only an occasional word through the onslaught.

'. . . your medicine . . . potatoes . . . *Poll*ard,' she heard.

She heard the word 'Grandmamma' followed by a crooning like a lullaby. She is quite mad, Rowena thought sadly.

She waited. She ran her fingernails lightly under the beading, crouched down, and when the rain was at its most torrential, she pushed the section of tongue-and-groove very gently until it opened a little.

For a few seconds, she watched what she could see of Eva, a thin and dirty-haired girl leaning over the bottom shelf in that choking cupboard, now close and dark with rain.

'Sweet Grand*mamm*a,' she said, and she seemed to be rubbing the bedding on the shelf. 'You need to *stay* warm.' She was leaning over the lower bunk, and there were more murmurings barely audible to Rowena.

'Eva,' said Rowena gently.

Eva screamed. In one movement, she stretched herself further over the bed, yanked an eiderdown over the pillows, then stood in front of the wadded shelf with its unseemly heap of bedclothes. She stayed there, visibly trembling.

'Thank God,' said Rowena in a croaky whisper. The room was cooler yet ever thicker with sour odours. She saw the canary behind glass, now listing so its lumpy body was bent almost double, and jolted away.

'Eva?' She took Eva into her arms, covering her head with kisses. 'Come down,' she said, pushing her towards the door. Rain pelted the skylight.

'I will return,' said Eva as they left.

'No, you will not,' said Rowena quite fiercely.

'*Je Reviens*,' said Eva very clearly.

'My God,' said Rowena. 'That. That — perfume. You sound — you sound quite *mad*. Don't, don't darling. This has got to stop.'

On the landing, Rowena pulled Eva to her again, and Eva lay her head against her mother's shoulder. Rowena stroked her hair.

'Come back to us, Eva,' she said. 'You're so thin. My darling, you are so thin. Please. What are you *doing* up here? This horrible, horrible old room.'

Eva smiled. She shook her head.

'Have you seen Jennifer?' said Rowena in a low voice.

'No,' said Eva.

'Really?' said Rowena, her voice catching in her throat. 'Are you sure?'

'I'm sure.'

Rowena nodded slowly, her head heavy.

For the first time in many months, Eva put her arms around her mother. 'I am here,' she said in her low slow voice. 'That *means* Jennifer will come back too.'

'How can I know that?' said Rowena, but a hope rose through her.

After a bath and a meal that she ate in hungry silence, Evangeline stood up quite abruptly and began to walk out of the room.

'Where are you going?' said Rowena.

'I need to go back up,' said Eva, and began to hurry towards the staircase.

'You do not,' said Rowena, following and putting her hand on Eva's shoulder. 'Sit down on the sofa. You are *not* going up to that horrible creepy cupboard.'

'I need to,' said Eva, a hard expression appearing on her face.

'Certainly not,' said Rowena with fresh force. 'Sit down. Tell me. Tell me *now*, Eva, where you've been all this time.'

Eva smiled. 'In the fields, Mother.'

'You've been here, haven't you? You've been in that room?'

'I need to get back up there.'

'You are not going up there.'

'I need to look after her. She can't be on her own.'

'*Who?*

'*She can't.*'

'Jennifer?' said Rowena with a cry.

Eva shook her head slightly. Pity crossed her face.

'*Who?*' said Rowena again, tears sliding down her cheeks without restraint.

Eva reached up and wiped them.

'Grand*mamm*a,' she said simply.

Rowena stared at Eva. She drew in her breath. 'Eva,' she said in a fast furious growl. 'Do you not realise what you're saying? What are you saying? What are you talking about? This is *illness*—'

Eva shrugged.

'Well?' snapped Rowena.

'What could I do?' said Eva. 'She only wanted to *stay* in her house.'

'This is ancient history, Evangeline.' Rowena felt heat rush to her head.

'But how – how could I not help *to* keep her at home? How could I let you push her out of her home when all her heart wanted was to be *at* her own, own home and she needed help?'

'Eva, Eva!' Rowena was shouting. 'Stop! Stop! You sound *mad*. Don't you realise? If you talk like that, they will take you away. Darling. How long have you spent up there?'

'I've been *looking* after Grandmamma,' said Eva in a low steady voice. 'Feeding her, talking to her, sewing, mending—'

'You've been up there, hiding up there, all this time?'

Eva said nothing.

'Oh God,' said Rowena. 'Those noises.' She reached across, and took Eva's wrists, holding them so hard that Eva pulled them away. 'They will think you're mad.'

'Who *will*?'

'Everyone. The police. Doug – Daddy. Everyone, everyone. They will put you away if you say things like that, don't you understand?' She clutched her again, urgently.

'I'm being shut away anyway,' said Eva sulkily.

'What do you mean?'

'Of course *I* am.'

'Oh – Ragdell.' Rowena took a deep breath. 'No, no, darling,' she said more gently. 'Much worse than that. You speak like that and they'll put you in – I don't know – a reform school, institution, somewhere where they can help you. Treat you. ECG. I don't know—'

Eva shrugged. 'She needs feeding, changing, lov—'

'You must not SAY this stuff. You are not understanding me. This isn't normal. They'll give you – I don't know – a lobotomy. Don't you see? And if you say these things to the police, perhaps, perhaps they will not return Jennifer to us either when they find her. They won't think we are suitable parents.'

'I *would* never tell the police,' said Eva in a hiss. 'Anyway. Grandmamma needs protecting.'

'Good God, Eva. This is the very last time you will tell these stupid tales. This is a diseased fantasy. You must, must stop, darling.'

'I know exactly what I am telling the police of my where*abouts*,' Eva said calmly. 'Which meadow, dwelling, field and garden I have been staying in. I planned it all out in our room.'

Rowena shook her head, her jaw slack.

'Where is Jennifer?' she said.

'I don't know, I don't know, I don't know.'

The front door opened to the noise of a torrent from the gutter.

'Have the police called since lunch?' came Douglas's voice, the urgency in his tone audible.

'Yes,' answered Rowena. 'But nothing to report. Eva is ba—' she called before he came into the main room, instinct warning her, but he was already there and staring at Eva.

Eva had struggled to her feet, her eyes like a dazed sea creature's beneath the plastered water-rat hair of her bath.

He strode over and hit her on the cheek.

'Douglas!' shrieked Rowena. She leapt up and tugged him away from where Eva was now standing, her eyes wide with shock. 'Douglas!' she cried, and she grabbed his arm.

Eva opened her mouth, turned, and ran upstairs, a thin battered figure, more ghostly than she had ever been.

'I think I *hate* you,' Rowena said to her husband.

16

The Pollards were on their annual holiday to Wales but the police wanted to inspect Brinden without further delay, and Rosemary knew where the spare key was hidden.

Early the next morning, Rowena and Rosemary accompanied the police while a lady officer was booked to interview Evangeline at The Farings. The rain had stopped, but the police van skidded on the path, and the overgrown nettles, docks and bushes soaked their legs on the path to the side door. Rowena had never seen so many snails; the large cats mewled in a chorus, aggressively rubbing against their legs until Rosemary stumbled. She had brought food for Rosie and Ginger, but when she laid it in front of them, there was a hissing, spitting fury of cats, a yowling of torn ears and despair.

'We must bring them more, Mummy,' said Rosemary. 'Especially Ginger. I have to look after him for Jennifer. Meribell went away quite quickly. I think she died. Poor Eva.'

The house was silent, shuttered and dark, marginally tidier in the cluttered areas, but cheerless in a fashion neither of them had seen before. Fly nets were placed over plates of dried meat and fruit, now browning. Seedlings left on a windowsill were drooping. Rowena picked her way through the semi-cellar rooms at the back of the house, over lawnmower parts, tools and rusting containers, oil staining her legs as she clambered through the warren of storage spaces she had previously navigated, but she could no longer find the door to the pink bedroom. It wasn't where she had remembered it; there was only a wall where she had thought the door would be, and the mangle was elsewhere, the tricycle nowhere to be seen, and she was uncertain about her orientation. She returned a different way to where she thought the pantry was, and came out through a door to the kitchen yard instead.

Rowena found Mrs Pollard's dining room, where the oil portrait of Jennifer jumped out at her in the gloom, and she began to cry again. 'It is *wrong*,' she said. 'Oh, Rosemary, don't look.' But Rosemary was crying too, sobbing red-faced as she rarely did. They cried together, clutching each other as the police began their search. The house and grounds were too big to inspect in one day, they said, and they would work until nightfall, then call in more officers the following day to comb the entire place if necessary.

'I *do* not,' said Evangeline at The Farings, sitting on the sofa in her grandmother's dress and pinafore, kicking up one leg after the other and revealing the trim of her gored petticoat until she was frowned at.

The lady policeman was asking her lots of questions that she could answer very easily, although she was grilled extensively and the police officer thought it fit to chide her for the suffering imposed on her mother. Eva sat up straight and answered in her level chalky voice. She had been sleeping in the fields and gardens all around, she said; it was so hot, so airless inside. She missed her grandmother, and her parents should not have taken her house and knocked down her wall. She was very angry with them for that; so angry, she would rather avoid them. She had spent some time at the Pollards'. Had she seen Jennifer there? Yes, her sisters had played there in the past, and she had seen Jennifer there recently. How often did she see Jennifer? Not often. How would she describe Jennifer's character? It was hard to say: she was quiet, undemanding, but of a sunny disposition. 'All any*one* ever notices about her is how *she* looks,' said Eva. 'It is all about her.'

She was questioned for over three hours. She managed not to address Freddie, recalled all the answers she had prepared, and was twice asked to repeat details of her whereabouts, itemising nights spent at Brinden, in woods, sheds, hedges and the garden, demonstrating a consistency that finally satisfied the officer.

Rowena returned and talked to the police officer as Rosemary made cups of tea, awkwardly placing an arm around her crying mother, while Evangeline disappeared upstairs. There were new framed pictures on the walls of her grandmother's staircase, Eva noticed, a modern jagged black-and-white rug on the landing. She spat on it, and rubbed the spittle in with her foot.

Bob emerged from his room and wrapped his arms about her, laughing. 'I seen Freddie more van you, Evie!'

Evangeline looked down at his round eyes gazing up at her. She tousled his hair and bit her lip.

'Have you, *Bob*?'

'Yus yus. When you away, Freddie here!'

'You *looked* after Freddie?'

'I like Freddie.'

'Yes, Bob. I haven't seen Freddie for *an* age.'

'I *sees him*,' said Bob.

'I don't. Where?'

'By Mummy's back. Kitchen. Here. I like Freddie!'

'Yes,' said Eva. 'What does he look *like*? How old is he?'

Bob shrugged.

'Smaller than you?'

'Bigger,' said Bob firmly, nodding.

'Bigger or smaller *than* me?'

'Bit — bit smaller.'

'Who does he like most?'

'Mummy,' said Bob instantly.

Child Actress Vanishes, said the headline, accompanied by a still from *Blush* in which a widening effect of the lens flattened Jennifer's face, and, as in the film, lent her an almost ordinary appearance. In black-and-white, her hair's blondeness could have been mouse toned, and the eyes that had seemed to possess an almost worrying glare in the footage were unremarkable in the still.

Brinden was revisited, fields and woods as far as

Epping searched; every rally driver who had gathered in the village at the time of Jennifer's disappearance was interviewed and profiled.

There was, thought Rowena, quite simply spite in The Farings. Could they really live in this village where the house turned against them and they lost children? Dreams, already shattered, were irretrievable: it was the nightmare now that she fought.

The walls on either side of the arch between the two houses were openly flaunting their canker, the ceiling opening slowly in brown-ringed sections of plaster. Sometimes rooms were bathed with *Je Reviens*; at other times, decay dominated. The wallpaper was furry with bulges of mould, as though mice ran under it. In a previous period, the decomposition would have made Rowena despair. Now it merely formed the backdrop to chaos as the past soaked in.

Eva's absences increased once again, but now she would appear just as her mother showed signs of agitation.

She crept down the stairs, her stockinged feet making no noise, but Rowena grabbed her as she entered the main room.

'You must stay at home more!'

'Do *not* worry about me,' said Eva. 'I am safe. It's the summer.'

'But where do you go?'

Eva gazed. 'Same,' she said, her lips' stubborn set momentarily silencing Rowena. Rather than her usual dress, petticoats and pinafore, she was wearing an elaborate lace blouse with a long skirt that was too big for her.

Rowena gave an exasperated sigh. 'You will look for Jennifer?'

Eva nodded.

'Everywhere?'

'Yes.'

'*Everywhere* you go, Eva. Call and search.'

'Yes, *I'll* look.'

'Eva,' Rowena called just as Evangeline was leaving. She turned, clasping her skirt at the waist. 'How did you *know* Jennifer had disappeared?'

'I didn't,' said Eva.

'But you did. When—'

'When?'

'When I found you. You knew. You comforted me and said not to worry.'

'Oh, I—' said Eva, and she paused.

'You know something,' Rowena said, her voice catching.

Eva dropped her gaze. When she looked up, her eyes glistened.

'No, Mummy.'

'You never call me "Mummy". What is it you know? You must *tell* me.'

Eva paused for the smallest fragment of time.

'I heard you calling for her from upstairs. I don't know where she is,' she said. 'But I'm sure *she's* safe.'

Later in the day, Rowena lay on the floor gazing at the ceiling as Bob had his nap and Rosemary played with the post office children. The night had once more been devoid of sleep, Rowena only dozing just before the alarm went, then turning sick with tiredness to her pillow to cry. The ceiling sagged. Do your worst, she thought. If it fell on her, it would take away all pain and all fear. There was a tap from upstairs, a rush, a burp of sound, and a stain moved over the ceiling in front of her eyes to meet others, so slowly, so slowly she was barely certain, and she smelled again the cat's urine, along with the scent. She could, she noticed, only detect the perfume at certain times of the month.

She willed the stain further, her head fuzzy. Fall on me, she thought. She heard Greg's car door slam outside. She knew when he arrived home at lunchtime – he said he preferred his wife's cooking to the canteen sludge, and that anxious, good plain wife was always ready in a pinny – just as she knew the time he swung out again, his jacket over his shoulder, spinning his hat on to the seat beside him.

She lay there and felt herself a little, longing for him as tears rolled down the sides of her face. The walls seemed to creep in on her. Squash me, she thought. There was a knock on the door, and she turned her head but didn't get up. A cockerel cried outside, at the wrong time of day, and water shimmered in the corner.

'Rowena?' called Gregory softly. He inched open the door. 'Rowena.'

'In here,' she said.

The sun pattered in tentative warmth over the tiles, and there he was, immensely tall above her.

'"She loosed the chain, and down she lay,"' he said. 'How exquisite you are, Lady Crale.'

She smiled up at him. 'You are beautiful,' she said, barely moving her mouth.

He knelt beside her and stroked her feet, trailing his fingers up her calves so she shivered. He stroked her for a long time. She tried to pull him closer, but he resisted, lingering on her thighs, playing, tickling, holding back, occasionally dipping to kiss the crook of her elbow and her neck until she grasped him.

'Patience, Lady Crale,' he said, murmuring right inside her ear. 'I want to kiss the freckles on your haughty nose. Your hair is ember-coloured in the sun. Your figure is the finest I have ever seen. Patience.'

'No,' she moaned.

'No one here?' he said, feeling in his pocket.

She shook her head. All she wanted, she thought, was him inside her right now, hard and insistent, ridding her of loss, of guilt, of misery, of everything. He plunged into her and she cried out and she was alive; she was alive. She loved him.

'We could make this a regular meeting,' he said afterwards. 'Suddenly I have developed a taste for the power station's reconstituted shepherd's pie.'

'Oh yes. Yes.'

'Every day at ten past one. We will find places to be together. To do . . . whatever you need to do until your daughter comes back.'

'Oh, Greg. I – I think I lo—'

'Hush now,' he said, and she froze.

'I love you, Lady Crale,' he called as he closed the front door, and she lay there in the sun.

She will come back, she whispered to herself.

She allowed the little boy to be in the other room, to make a shadow on the corner of her eye. Then, for the first time, she called him to her, and tried to embrace him, but he hovered next door and wouldn't come.

She lay there with just her mind to play with till Bob woke. She thought about John Profumo, about the Russian and the osteopath and their women, as she had from the start of the scandal. Every day she scoured the papers for more to distract her for a few minutes at a time. Even Mr Kennedy, it seemed, cheated on that lovely wife of his with actresses and strippers. They were more immoral than her, the whole lot of them.

Or were they? She might make love with a married man, but a worse guilt hooked her and inhabited her. She was haunted by an old lady she had wronged and by children she had lost. She felt a little hand in hers, and pulled Freddie to her.

17

There was still no Jennifer, only police and journalists, nosy neighbours and more questions, and a house that made a mockery of its inhabitants.

Douglas Crale threw himself into his work, travelling to London early each morning, then ranting by telephone to the police and Rowena. Rowena moved in a daze, and all that kept her breathing and fighting was Gregory Dangerfield. Intimacy blanked out reality. He invented any number of meetings and research trips, and during those times, she began to leave Bob with the pensioner three doors down who had been friends with Mrs Crale. She seemed to look at Rowena askance but was kind to Bob and let him watch *Andy Pandy* with his snack.

*

'You're back, Mr Pollard,' said Evangeline, who was making enough appearances at home to keep her parents calm. Jumping out at him from the bushes, she skipped beside him as he made his way from his old farm van along the path to his back door at Brinden.

'Chickabiddy,' said Pollard with a smile, his blue eyes scanning the distance, his dancer gait graceful even as he carried a sack of cement.

'Oh, I *am* your favourite!' said Eva. 'I hope I am, I am, not *that* Jennifer with her dimple.' She laughed.

'Have an apple. You are the one I knew from the start, silly missy, so remember it.'

'*Be*fore the start, Pollard,' said Eva primly. 'Oh, Pollard, you are the only one who understands! They all think I have mostly *been* wandering the lanes like a vagrant and gypsy. Even the lady policeman believed it all.'

'You're a naughty one. Hush now, Eva. I needs to see the missus, then I will set you a new treasure hunt. There's lots you haven't found already, even with your nosy ways.'

'What? What?'

'Plenty. There's a tree platform hidden. There's washrooms, more tool sheds and lofts, more gates behind bramble patches. Here's a bet you haven't found all the yards. A Caramac for every new bit you find.'

'Oh, I love it here so much, Mr Pollard. When I am with dear Grand*mamma*, I wonder to myself what is going on in lovely wild Brinden.'

They reached the shed, where they smoked a cigarette, poured plastic into petal moulds for the roses, and jiggled to 'From Me to You'. Eva sat and watched him as he cooked them a fried breakfast, and planned what she would take back for her grandmother.

'I must return to Grandmamma soon,' she said, and Pollard, prodding the tomatoes, nodded.

As he cooked, the wireless blaring, she pictured her grandmother, an old lady like a poor lost child almost fading away, blue-veined and withered among all the lace and eiderdowns on the shelf bunk they had made for her. She had to prop her up at times, lift her bird-like weight, feed her with a spoon, cradle her and stroke her, bathe her from a washstand with stolen warm water. The previous cat had died, but Meribell was there to keep her company, the clouds through the skylight their friends.

'You know, Pollard,' Eva said, tripping over the speed of her words, 'she is very *fine*. She reads *every* book that was ever written. *She* grew up in Kensington. She knows what is precious and worthy. She *can* make real lace! She is more precious to me than my own life, Mr Pollard, and I will always look after her. May I take her a lettuce today from the garden?'

Pollard nodded as he nodded at almost everything, accepting all. 'Whenever you want. Them cats need feeding,' he said, jerking his head at a mewling pack outside the window. 'We'll throw 'em some bacon bits.'

'I love you, Pollard!'

'That's as may be,' said Pollard phlegmatically.

Rowena and Gregory met almost daily. They had sex, they drank, they drove, weaving about the lanes. They went flying. Perhaps, Rowena thought, it was marvellous after all, this village where there was an aerodrome and a handsome man in a hat to take you along tree-lined lanes up to the skies, sozzled, while the wife was at home. Lana Dangerfield stayed inside her house, kept trim, baked, held Tupperware parties and visited old ladies. Sometimes, Rowena made love with Gregory in his shed, and once the Tuesday gardener came upon them as they entered it, but Lana saw nothing and Douglas appeared not to notice, even when Rowena put the children to bed early, drove herself to meet Greg for dinner and pretended she was at a yoga exercise class to keep herself slender. They would sit over candles and steak, and, practical and eternally optimistic, he would listen slightly more than most men ever did as she talked at him about Jennifer and cried against his shirtsleeve. Successful in subterfuge, they became more careless.

'You've had others, haven't you?' she said to him one day.

He raised his eyebrow in enquiry.

'Other girlfriends. Since you've been married. *Mistresses*.'

His mouth visibly tightened, despite the playfully arched brow. 'Yes,' he said, tapping his finger on the table.

She gave a small smile. 'At least you're honest. Many?'

'What's many? No.'

'So I am the latest. The newcomer to the village. The new toy.'

'No, you're not,' he said.

She said nothing.

'You know that,' he said.

They were silent.

He kissed her in full public view in the restaurant, igniting the head rush of desire, but then the face of Jennifer came to her once again, and beyond her, Mrs Crale. They bobbed, two faces, one in front of the other, and she gasped a little, fear reaching out to claw at her so his lips on hers were cold moving things, meaning nothing.

'Jennifer,' she said abruptly, pulling apart from him. 'Oh, Jennifer.' She tried to hide her face.

'Your girl,' he said gently, and he placed his hand behind her back and pulled her to him. 'She will come back. The other one did,' he said, pressing her shoulders, her neck, rubbing her vigorously as though she were a dog or one of his children, and she sat limply as he stroked her, and leaned her head against him.

'Oh, Greg,' she said. 'You are what I need. You know that, don't you?' She gazed into his eyes.

'I hope so. And yet I'm not sure . . . that the world would agree with us, Lady Crale.'

'I know, I know,' she said hastily. The faces melted, and she kissed him.

Jennifer Crale did not return all summer. The search flared up in the press, reaching a crescendo with the release of *Blush*, Lally Lyn finding herself quite unable not to offer up a comment. Douglas bellowed about the police, about the detective, about Rowena, about the press, about the county, about Evangeline, about anyone but himself, until Rowena was in tears, and as the light fell, she made her bedroom dark and gazed across the garden from her window at Gregory's house, hoping to catch a glimpse of him upstairs; but she so rarely did, and frequently she had to turn away at the sight of Lana tidying, watching.

Freddie was observing her just as Lana was, but he was talking and playing noiselessly, more fearful of her than she was of him. He was reflected in the other window when she turned from the Dangerfield house, a figure of a boy in shorts and shirt bending over, occupied with something in his hand. He was losing some of his timidity. She tried to summon him to her bed to hold him, a comfort to her even as she was trying to nurture him, but he stood back in the shadows where she could barely detect him and watched her.

With Jennifer gone, the Crales huddled, muted, in the number 2 side of the house with its breakfast bar, its brave swirls of red and orange, while the number 3 side belched and sagged, screws on joists pressing through the plaster, a beam rotting, paint soft with spores.

On dull mornings when Rowena wandered through the house, she was aware that Freddie was showing his presence more in ways she could barely fathom, only a certainty that she was seen and sometimes followed informing her. He came to her more as the summer wore on, like a wild creature shaking off its shyness, the effect of his presence cumulative. At times, he was a glimmer on the lens, waiting in the shadows, lurking beneath the bed, brooding in the darkness. Once she almost felt his kiss.

For the first time, she acknowledged that he was more than the invention of poor crazed Evangeline. This boy was real. But she hadn't wanted him. She hadn't wanted him, and her body had made him die. His name was . . . ? He hadn't even had a name.

Words, mannerisms, memories would rush into that damp room with its perfume and mould: the faces of creatures who were her punishment. They all crowded around her when she was alone, when she wasn't embracing or soaking Gregory Dangerfield with tears. Jennifer was a constant awareness in the form of a two-dimensional picture, a physical being who was vital but not there. It was the other two, the young and old, who followed her, one courting her, the other spiting her. They shuffled around her. They followed, then silently scurried away when she looked, figures caught at the side of her eye. She smelled her mother-in-law, almost heard her, a babble, a croak absorbed by the damp of the ceiling. Just how hungry had she been? How thin? How determined?

And the boy appeared. Sometimes he smelled of stream water and she longed to towel him down, but his shape eluded her grasp; at times she smelled orange ice lollies; on other days, he had grubby hair, or he had been playing with sulphurous caps from a toy gun. He was cheerful and self-contained, but at times of sadness she smelled his tears, the scent of salty grief wetting hot cheeks, and she felt hollow with the longing to hold him. He was the missing child, the one who had never had a chance of life. She had seen him, tiny, frozen and dead, and now she saw him again.

18

It was almost the end of the summer holidays, the hay was gathered, and Evangeline was at Brinden in a floral dress of her grandmother's that hadn't previously fitted, unevenly tightened at the bodice seams.

She was visiting Pollard, who was painting Jennifer as he had all summer, and she handed him his palette. Jennifer's hair was pinned to the top of her head in Tyrolean plaits; she wore a dirndl that Mrs Pollard had run up and, as ever, fine cotton gloves. Mrs Pollard was making new outfits almost daily on her old machine on a table in the garden shelter, calling out to the babies in her cream-puff voice. Rigid in her frock, Eva cut her eye from Jennifer as she soaked brushes in turpentine, arranged colours at Pollard's request, and found him the brushes he tucked behind his ear or held in his mouth, while he issued instructions to Jennifer on how to pose. Ginger the cat thumped open the shed door with her sizeable weight and wound around Jennifer's legs, which was tolerated only if she stood still, but at times Jennifer's eyes glistened as though the sun had caught the surface of the blue lakes that Pollard persistently attempted to capture.

While he was still painting, the police made one of their regular visits. He carried on working for a few minutes, humming to Herb Alpert while Mrs Pollard greeted the officers in a friendly fashion and invited them in for her seed cake.

'Into me art cupboard, Jenn'fer,' said Pollard comfortingly, and placed his portrait of her beneath another canvas, starting to work on a different painting without a pause.

Eva sat on his pile of newspapers on a chair, smoking and kicking out one leg beneath her lacy layers. She wore her red flannel petticoat even though it was summer, because it was a favourite.

'Now we can talk,' she said.

'I'll fry us up a bacon platter,' he said. 'Save some for the other one for when the busybodies have cleared off my land.'

Eva giggled.

'They brought in a dog last time, but the mutt

went wild with all the cats here,' he said, winking, then frowning at a tree he was painting. He lit them both another cigarette and placed a chunk of lard in his pan. 'Lovely fresh tomatoes from the missus's garden too. Put that ciggie out for the minute, Eva.

'Have the run of the place,' said Pollard as the police arrived at the door. 'The girl's sister is here. Been mighty upset. But she's learning flower making.'

Plastic petals softened on Pollard's workbench. A few minutes later, Evangeline and Jennifer downed an afternoon fried breakfast while the police spent several hours searching the house once more, noting the presence of baby Caroline Crale and spending a further hour at Mrs Pollard's table with her largest teapot and most of a seed cake.

'Have your fill, my dears. Jennifer always did like Battenberg best,' she said sadly.

Mrs Pollard had provided Jennifer with her own fashionable wicker swing chair which she erected in the shelter in the garden beside a pile of modern girls' magazines, and after feeding her a large lunch with a glass of milk, she read to her and rocked her to sleep as the babies napped. In the afternoons, she set up the hairdressing salon and arranged Jennifer's hair however Mr Pollard most liked it for his paintings.

'I thought I was your *favourite*, Pollard,' Evangeline hissed.

'Course you are, chickabiddy,' said Pollard with his usual ease.

'Well, why don't you paint me more?'

'I'm doing a series of young Jenn'fer,' he said, and there was no argument.

Eva assisted with the props and the outfits that Mrs Pollard's hairstyles completed, and Jennifer stood there gazing like a shop dummy.

Eventually, Jennifer left to go inside the house, carrying flowers to take to Mrs Pollard.

It had been easy for Mr Pollard to hide Jennifer at Brinden with all its rooms and turns and hidden dark places, yet he barely needed to use those odd levels, those coal holes and weed-grown caravans, which were more obvious. When the police searched, he merely moved Jennifer from room to room with an almost casual ease; at times, she, Eva and Pollard would be chatting in quiet voices, winking and stifling giggles, and the police would be two rooms away. The house was scattered with her old finger-prints alongside Eva's and Rosemary's, but she kept her cotton gloves on like an obedient child even on those blazing August days. Pollard painted her many times, presenting each precious portrait to his wife with pride, and Jennifer would weep for her mother until she was told it was more *fun* at Brinden, Jennifer; and then the tears – the tears in the blue eyes that Pollard would quickly sketch – would dry, and she would play with the babies and treat Brinden as the adventure playground it was.

'Beautiful, Jenn'fer, beautiful,' Mr Pollard would say encouragingly as he painted her, and Eva scowled as she helped or went back with an extra meal wrapped up in her pockets.

Now Eva leaned against Pollard, her lace collar picking up paint from his shirt, but he didn't move. He laughed at her. 'You're my little odd one,' he said.

She smiled. 'You always wanted her here,' she said.

'That's right.'

'Do I look like Jennifer?' she said after a while.

'Now, why would you be asking me that? You know you don't.'

'What do I *look* like?'

'Like a grey little cat with shark-creature's eyes. Like a funny little missy.'

'And what does Jennifer look like?'

'Like God's own work.'

Eva flinched as though she had been slapped.

'But he forgot her mind while he was making her,' said Pollard.

✻

That night, Rowena was sleepless again even through the thick blanket of her pills. She remembered Jennifer at Brinden in happier days, and Jennifer's reticence after her sighting of Eva there, and however many times the police had searched, she was still suspicious of the place and its owners. But when she had informed the police of the partially complete girl's room and attempted to show them where it was, she had again found nothing but a wall, this time with shelves attached to it, and the pair of officers had reacted in a polite manner that seemed to imply they were humouring an unstable mother through her fantasy.

She shivered, glanced at Douglas who was sleeping deeply, murmured to Freddie in case he was in the shadows, dressed, and walked the long way, round starlit lanes, their cottages hunched, towards Brinden, which lay as a long indistinct spread of buildings across fields. Two windows were lit upstairs; the rest of the house sat in darkness. Instead of taking the path past the caravan to the back door that the Pollards used, Rowena approached from the side, making her way towards the garden, cats immediately winding themselves around her legs and following her. She passed darkened windows, her heart speeding in case she was seen by the Pollards or shot at like a dog. She rounded a corner of the garden and there, several feet from her, was a lamplit window alcove, and behind the glass in the depths of the room glowed the face of Jennifer, composed in all her beauty.

Rowena let out a small scream. She stumbled towards the window. Jennifer's face was strangely still as she gazed out from behind the low lamplight, further lit by two candles inside the room, and Rowena slid on gravel so her knee bled, then scrambled to her feet, and even before she got to the window, she realised. The face that floated disembodied behind the lamp belonged not to Jennifer, but to a portrait of her, illuminated in that dark room by two candles whose flames spread their gold light beneath the painting.

Rowena wanted to smash her face against the glass. 'Oh God,' she cried. 'Jennifer. This is not *right*.'

She bellowed, rapping on the window, protesting, and all along she thought she heard the voice of Jennifer, sobbing from far off, but she knew it was only her own catching breaths, and eventually Mrs Pollard came down in a dressing gown and enormous curlers, smelling of sour milk, and clutched Rowena to her breast.

Mr Pollard followed and loitered in the shadows.

'*Why* are you painting my daughter?' said Rowena, spitting out her words.

'Oh — it is a kind of shrine to her, dear,' said Mrs Pollard, gazing with her round unblinking eyes.

And Rowena turned and saw further pictures through the semi-darkness of a room peopled by slightly skewed Jennifers, recognisable but wrong in ways that were hard to define.

'She's not *dead*,' she shouted.

The Pollards looked kindly and slightly doubtful.

'We keep the candles burning,' was all Mrs Pollard said.

'Have the police seen this?'

'Well, of course,' said Mrs Pollard softly. 'They admire my Arthur's handiwork, and they sometimes have their tea in here so we can focus on dear Jennifer. "She is so beautiful," they always say,' she added, and in her voice Rowena detected an undisguisable note of pride.

19

The next morning, Rowena watched the green, jumping at blonde hair, at any girl of Jennifer's height, and waited for Gregory Dangerfield's lunchtime visit. She had grown reckless. It seemed to her almost certain that Douglas would have noticed them together, and yet he appeared to remain oblivious, working all hours in London, talking to the police, and returning late. The village gossiped about her, she realised. She had replaced Lally Lyn as the principal subject of conjecture, but it was of little concern.

She saw Eva sometimes, a shabby wraith on the green as autumn wept, while the boy always played around her on the periphery of her awareness, slipping between rooms, approaching her only from behind to tug with his eyes. He played games with her, scurrying and ruffling the air, then hiding in the shadows. She felt him laughing as she tried to find him.

Eva sat in the tiny Victorian room, doing her lace-making and tatting and working on an elaborate sampler of the green for her grandmother, whom she addressed as she sewed, singing, soothing and chatting.

She could never have kept her grandmother in her home without Arthur Pollard's collusion, she thought. Accepting all that he was told without question, he had cleared that old airing cupboard, covered over the doorway and suggested fashionable long wood panels to Rowena Crale before the family had arrived; then Eva had filled it with the objects her dear grandmother had treasured over so much time, and dedicated countless hours to its decoration, covering it all with the dust she had gathered.

The plotting had started the Easter that Douglas and Rowena had broached their plans to send old Evangeline away and move into her house. Over the school holidays, Eva had stayed at number 3 The Farings and looked after her grandmother, who was unable to eat in her shock. They plotted, whispered, talked all through the holidays as old Evangeline grew thinner. *They would create their own happiness*, they said.

'I remember you when you was so high – a little missy in frocks and lace and ribbons,' Pollard said a few hours later when Eva had arrived at Brinden in search of fresh food.

'*Only* I stayed with Grand*mamma* in the school holidays,' said Eva proudly. 'She gave me her clothes because *we* are almost one person.'

'That's right.'

'And you, *Poll*ard, you always did more work for her than you needed to, and for that, how can I ever thank you?'

'No need to now, missy. You did help me, didn't you?'

Eva turned away.

Pollard laughed. 'My little outcast. You're the black sheep like me, chickabiddy,' he said cheerfully. 'We wrong 'uns find each other, and then there's no knowing what we do. Nothing to stop us, eh, missy?'

Eva laughed too, then she frowned. 'How can I *be* better?' she said.

'You can't be, my chickabiddy. I like you just the way you are.'

'But it's Jennifer you gaze at.'

'For my paintings.'

'I wish you would *paint* me.'

'It's you I want to talk to. You, my grey little

ghostie. I like an odd one. One day you will make a good man proud.'

'You! You!'

'None of that talk, now. You behave, missy.'

She hesitated. 'Yes, Pollard.'

'That one,' he murmured, tilting his head towards Jennifer's portrait, 'her head is full of nothing. Dull girl if you ask me, missy, and a bit strange in the head, but that's enough of that. Fetch me a couple of eggs and a few windfalls and we'll cook them up to go with our fried potatoes.'

In the garden, Jennifer dully fed the row of babies from their bottles, Ginger butting her and Mrs Pollard leaning over to kiss her head on her way to the kitchen.

'That woman has too many, and keeps losing them,' she would say, crooning and re-brushing Jennifer's hair.

Mrs Pollard kept an eye on Jennifer through the window as she always did, and made sure she never wandered from sight, while Jennifer sat captive in the cabbages playing with the Tressy doll Mrs Pollard had bought her and shivered a little. Autumn was scenting the air, and the babies now lay in a row covered in their yellow waffle blankets, while those beginning to crawl clambered unsteadily over the rockery in their jerseys.

'You,' said the oldest, due to leave that week: a mischievous one-year-old in a home-knit who had started to say a few words. She pointed at Jennifer.

'Yes?' said Jennifer, smiling down at her and taking her hand.

'You the curl,' she said.

'Curl?' She frowned. 'Do you mean – girl?'

'Yes! Curl!'

'I'm the girl?' said Jennifer, looking vacant.

The toddler nodded vigorously, gurgling with laughter. She danced around Jennifer a little, clinging to her legs, and tugged insistently at her mother's sleeve on collection.

Rowena was at home watching the green, as was her habit, looking for Jennifer. One day, she thought; one day soon, she prayed, Jennifer would emerge as Evangeline had.

Eva returned and spent the night in the small room, working on the sampler, chatting, and arranging the food she had brought from Brinden on dainty crockery for her grandmother; but poor pregnant Meribell was unwell, so as the birds woke, she made her way across the fields in the cold thin light, stumbling on flint and puddingstone, to ask Pollard what remedy she should use and whether Meribell was ready to kitten.

Brinden appeared to shimmer in the dawn, gold seeping into blue, and Eva looked forward to the bacon and eggs Pollard would fry her in his shed before she returned, but as she came closer, she saw vehicles there in the dip of land. The house and its immediate surroundings were ringed with tape, and a figure Eva recognised as the lady policeman who had interviewed her was standing stiffly outside the back door.

Eva froze, then ran across the rest of the field, tripping and weeping with fear, crawled under the tape and went straight to Pollard's shed.

His paints were out by his easel; the air was hung with fresh bacon fat, and blue roses were lined up on his workbench waiting for their stems, but there was no note for her, no sign.

She screamed, scanning the horizons, calling his name, then she put her head on the bench and cried more loudly than she ever had, except once.

They had all escaped, said the police. Mr and Mrs Pollard had simply driven away with Jennifer, as though they had had forewarning. They interrogated Eva, and she sobbed and shouted and showed her ignorance during their questions. Later, as the sun touched the fields, and the trees shivered with bright morning, she lay on the ground and cried for what she had done. She spilled her grief and regret and called, '*Jennifer, Jennifer.*' She lay face down on the earth, her pinafore dirtied, her face smeared with mud and tears.

She had wanted to help Pollard because he had helped her, but now that they had taken Jennifer and gone, she most bitterly regretted it. She screamed and wept into the mud until it filled her mouth.

The day of the car rally, she had slipped out of the little room, hurried along the lane and found Jennifer behind the church, where she had been talking to the vicar's wife while the rest of the family went ahead. Jennifer had then lingered to watch the motor cars, that fresh early afternoon stained with petrol exhaust in all its milling and confusion. Eva took her by the hand and dragged her the long way, all around the lanes and the spinney, across the mud track, Jennifer protesting and whining about her lunch, to Brinden. She had brought the most beautiful girl the villagers had ever seen, and had given her to Pollard. He had always wanted Jennifer, Eva thought, and here she was as a gift, though Eva hated her, hated Jennifer for the way people were with her, hated her even as she loved her.

'Not for me,' said Pollard, nodding. 'I got me roses. I got you to talk to. For the missus. We'll paint her up nicely and give the missus some pictures.

She'll love that more than I can say. Come along, Jenn'fer.'

So Mrs Pollard, mother of none, had her Jennifer, the very loveliest girl she had ever met, the daughter she had always dreamed of, and she cosseted her and pampered her, fed her milk and rice puddings and cakes, rocked her to sleep in the wicker chair, then dressed her in her creations. And Jennifer, who always was a pliable girl, became more and more like the doll she so resembled, until she blinked, her rosebud mouth held open, more often than she spoke.

20

'This isn't the right direction for Finchley,' said Rowena, frowning at a road sign.

'I—' Douglas cleared his throat and tapped lightly on the wheel with his index finger. His mouth tensed. 'I just want to show you somewhere on the way,' he said. He smiled at her, slightly awkwardly.

Rowena glanced at her watch, that elegant little Chopard her mother-in-law had once given her, which she tried to wear every day. 'We need to be in the house before the removal vans arrive,' she said.

Her mind roamed anxiously through The Farings, now almost emptied. There were still a few pieces of furniture to be packed, but she wondered whether she had forgotten anything of importance. She went methodically through every room and its contents, and, for the first time in several weeks, she strayed into the Victorian airing cupboard. White hair seemed to be there above an eiderdown on the whiteness of the pillow; large sunken eyes turned to her in the mirror. She darted straight out again. Closing the tongue-and-groove behind her, she hoped to forget, in some balmy future, that vision. The house had done its worst at the end, with its urinous splashes and spores; the floor on the landing impassable; the leaks weighting the ceiling until it resembled a rain-drenched tent; faces pressing into her poor bruised mind. They had had to sell The Farings for almost nothing. But then they had got half the house for nothing: for nothing at all.

Within weeks of her arrival, the staff at Ragdell Place had recommended Evangeline's transferral to an ordinary grammar school, and so the children could be educated in London and there was nothing to keep them there.

When they left it, Crowsley Beck could not have been more beautiful. Artists came there to paint and photograph the green with its snow-lined ring of elms for Christmas cards. Another production company had been shooting there, Jennifer's absence an ache that couldn't be dulled as Rowena stared at the crew and remembered. The lamp posts were twined with holly; a Christmas tree had been erected on the green, its candles lit by the church's carol singers in the blue of the late afternoons; the low fences and the war memorial were capped with snow, the pub shone blue-green-red across the white, and the stream gurgled black behind. Door knockers bore wreaths, the post office featured an illuminated Nativity, and Gregory Dangerfield's sports car wore a bonnet.

Gregory had made a cash purchase on a tiny flat in a spot between the village and Finchley that he and Rowena had chosen for its anonymity. 'Welcome to the scandalous Lady Crale's love nest,' he said, carrying her into it and leaning over the bed to kiss her.

The month before, Rowena had sat in the grey-green shadows by the window looking on to the grass. It was the day after the President was shot, and the pink suit kept coming into her mind. Builders were about to come in to dismantle the remains of the ceiling and examine the state of the joists. Was it worth it, she wondered dully? She knew the answer. Bob played a game that involved chasing around energetically by himself with a ball in the far side of the L-shaped room, while she merely sat listening to him. After a while, he stopped and all was quiet, and she knew that Freddie had left the game and crept beneath her skirt. If she looked down from the swivel lounge chair she sat on; if she challenged the busyness at the corner of her eye, the shadow would disappear less quickly now. It was becoming less shy. It was brushing her hem. He was the age he would have been had he lived.

It was her boy. She could admit it now, in grief, in longing for him in her arms.

She had been pregnant with another son and he had died before he was born, though no one talked about it at the time, and she had suffered in a guilty silence that wrapped her in something close to despair. She hadn't wanted to be pregnant again so quickly after the birth of the troubled infant who was her third daughter. She had held the protesting girl she had reluctantly named Evangeline, while clearing up after twins and vomiting with the new pregnancy, and she had taken baths until they were as scalding as she could tolerate, and bought gin to complete the job, and the cramps had started almost immediately, followed by the agony and mess. She had never told Douglas that the infant was a boy, but she had seen his body, and the pregnancy had been further advanced than she had known. When he was born, this tiny dead thing, he had a grazing of red hair, the only one of the Crale children to do so.

'I play with Freddie,' said Bob shyly to Rowena as she looked out at the green.

'Oh, Bob,' said Rowena. She straightened his hair, carefully. 'Are you sure?'

'I play with him just now!' said Bob. Bob the dog barked outside. Rowena stiffened.

'. . . OK, Bob,' she said gently.

'Then he come to you.'

Rowena paused.

'How?' she said.

'Come over to you. Here. He want to play with *you*, Mummy.'

Rowena gazed at the convex surface of the ceiling, pocked and stretched.

'What does Freddie look like?' she asked quietly as she drew Bob on to her lap to kiss his head, and he wriggled.

'Boy. Big boy.'

'Eva always said he was little,' said Rowena.

'No! Freddie here,' he said, lifting his hand in the air and holding it above him.

'And what – what else?'

'Nice. I like Freddie.'

'Good. What else does he look like? Darling?'

'Mmmm . . .' said Bob, shrugging. 'Hair orange!'

'Orange?' said Rowena, wonderingly. 'Red?'

Bob shrugged.

'A bit like mine?'

Bob knelt unsteadily on her lap and played with her hair. 'More more more orange!'

'I have to leave,' Rowena said to Douglas that evening when he came in from work, tossing his hat and scarf on the sofa and putting his feet up on the coffee table.

'Oh, Ro,' he said.

'Please. I don't want to live in this house any more.'

Douglas grunted. 'Get a chap a drink?'

'Of course,' said Rowena.

'You know, you know, Ro, it wouldn't be too bloody soon for me,' said Douglas, surprising her. 'The building costs will bankrupt me here.'

'Oh . . . ?' said Rowena.

'And that asinine Beeching will be closing so many of the branch lines, I've been wondering how I'll get in to work, unless I stay in digs in the week.' He sighed. 'I think we should sell up, Ro.'

Rowena looked away. 'I have to leave, and yet, and yet, I am leaving – him,' she whispered. 'Again.'

'Again? What are you talking about?'

Rowena flared a furious red and her eyes filled. The speed of her heart made her feel breathless.

'You know. He never leaves me.'

'Who the hell are you talking about, Rowena?' said Douglas, standing up suddenly and taking her by the shoulders.

'Him. The—'

'Are you trying to tell me what's bloody obvious?' shouted Douglas. 'You think I need telling?'

'You've seen him?'

'I thought you'd have the bloody grace to keep your dirty secrets to yourself. But no. Well, yes, by God, we *are* leaving.'

'Douglas, darling, please, please be kinder. I can't help it. He follows me, he haunts me. I can't – I don't know how to stop it – I—'

Douglas raised his hand, and he slapped her across the face.

Rowena was silent. She lifted her eyes. 'I will never forgive you for that,' she said in a quiet voice.

The horse-chestnut-arched lanes, the aerodrome, the private schools, the power station in its dip in the fields, all flew starkly past the car, winter-coloured, as they left Crowsley Beck. The children had gone ahead to the new house, dispiritingly similar to their former London home, supervised by Rowena's mother who had come up from Hampshire for the weekend to help.

'But *where* are we going?' said Rowena, frowning, as Douglas drove past a golf course and slowed the car. 'The removal vans may not be far behind us. Shenley, this says. This isn't the right way, is it?'

She could see Freddie reflected in the car windows, and pretended to apply her lipstick in the mirror so she could show him that she was checking on him. He was bouncing on the back seat in a restless re-arrangement of light. Once she thought she saw a movement behind him too, but it was nothing.

'Don't worry, Ro,' said Douglas. 'Darling,' he added with an unusual softness to his voice. He stopped the car in front of some large gates, swiftly got out and spoke to a security man in a booth, and the gates opened.

'Where *are* we?' said Rowena sharply as Douglas drove carefully through parkland. 'What on earth are you doing?'

'We just need to have a talk with Dr Singh,' said Douglas in the same gentle tones.

'Douglas, what do you mean?' said Rowena.

A turreted mansion, gracious but institutional, appeared at the end of the drive, nurses circling the front lawn in coats over uniforms, chaperoning people who were clearly psychiatric patients.

'Douglas!' shouted Rowena, grabbing the door handle, but a doctor was walking towards them with a welcoming smile.

The doctor held her gently by the arm and made

her stand, still smiling, and Rowena leaned over to wrench open the back door and let Freddie out. He took her hand with his little one as she tried to pull herself free of Dr Singh.

Just outside the main gates, Lally Lyn, the actress, popped up from the luggage space where she had hidden beneath a blanket, her tinkling laugh filling the car.

'Oh, darling!' she said. 'Oh, I so nearly gave myself away! This reminds me terribly of a play I was in years ago. I was a silly young thing, grotty little rep company. The mistress hid in the back of the car, then leapt up like a jack-in-the-box once the wife was out of the way. Oh, Doug sweetest, what a lark.'

She kissed the back of his neck and clambered into the front seat. 'Whoops!'

'I don't know that that felt altogether right,' said Douglas, stroking his chin. 'Though Dr Singh did say—'

'Oh, poor girl'll be much safer,' she said, touching up her lipstick in the mirror. 'You've been saying she's been going off her trolley almost since July. Let alone since ill-starred Jen. Now, let's plan a smashing Home Sweet Home picnic on the floor for the kids' supper!'

'Yes,' said Douglas absently, as the day began to

soften into twilight and he drove with an abstracted expression through country lanes that graded into suburbs. 'Darling,' he said, 'let's drive by my mother's grave. I never visit it. Right near here. I want to pay homage to the old girl.'

'Of course, my sweetheart,' said Lally. 'When did she die?'

'Just before we moved into The Farings, around Easter,' he said, slowing the car. 'It was pretty sad, the whole thing. I think Ro felt it badly. We were about to pack her off to live with her goddaughter or someone, all the way up in Inverness.'

'Heavens! The sticks.'

'Yes, well. The old girl was pretty past it, but she wanted to stay in her home, and I half think she died of a broken heart. Let herself starve before we could move her. I always felt a bit rotten. She was a dear.' He stopped the car. 'Here it is.'

'But I'm terribly puzzled,' said Lally, getting out of the car. 'Doug, darling, I saw her – well, I thought – only last night. I *assumed* it was your mother,' she said, frowning. 'She had the Crale eyes!'

'Don't be absurd, darling,' said Douglas, and tickled her so she giggled.

'Well, who was that old lady, then? I'm sure I've seen that *same* old dear a couple of times in the window upstairs, silly billy.'

'I have no idea,' said Douglas. 'Where? What kind of old lady, for heaven's sakes?'

'Clothes just like Eva's. Faded Victorian garb in the dusk. She was outside your house, looking up towards the window.'

NOW

I think Pollard is returning to me. He shows himself more and more; we watch each other.

'Who was your favourite?' I said to him when I finally saw him on my street.

He smiled. He was silent for a while.

'You know,' he said.

Pollard had simply left that day, and despite a massive search, he was never found. He abandoned me, and he didn't tell me how to find him. I wanted him and missed him for the rest of my childhood.

The police discovered Jennifer's pink room; they found all the portraits that had been hoarded for Mrs Pollard in case Jennifer was ever taken away from her, and they carted them out in piles, to be presented in the court case. If it hadn't been for the older baby who started speaking, Jennifer would have grown up there, at her home of Brinden.

Eventually, almost five years after the Pollards had escaped, Delyth Pollard was tracked down to a bungalow outside the Mumbles in Wales, where Jennifer was found pampered and confined, dressed in a playsuit, with her increasingly mousy hair back-combed into bunches. She was nursing a bloated Mrs Pollard, who had a tumour on her thyroid, and had begun to tut in impatience at her lethargic charge. Jennifer's childhood was over, and the somewhat fleshy seventeen-year-old with her flat face gazed vacantly with vast eyes when the police arrived. Mrs Pollard was arrested and sent to Holloway, where she died soon afterwards; Arthur Pollard was sentenced in his absence, while Jennifer was declared unfit to be returned to a home environment, and was sent instead as a weekly boarder to Ragdell Place.

Her eyes seemed to contain nothing. It was only after she returned that people hinted that she disturbed them with her doll face and her empty expression and her way of saying so little. The therapists at Ragdell said that Jennifer presented signs of capture-bonding, for she claimed that Mrs Pollard had loved her and Mr Pollard had been kind to her in her imprisonment. He never laid a finger on us, though the police, and much later the therapists, decided that he did. In her early twenties, Jennifer's celebrated looks made a partial return in the form of a puffy glamour, like a sedated actress's, and she began to live with a nurse she had met at Ragdell, who was besotted with her beauty.

Perhaps it is not always the strange ones who are strange.

When I think of our dear mother at Crowsley Beck, I remember her auburn fall of hair — in the sun on the green or catching the light as she gazed in hope out of the window. Even now, I cannot bear to think about what happened to her there.

Despite our neighbour Gregory Dangerfield's previous entanglements and the fact that he remained married for propriety, he claimed that Rowena Crale was his true love, and he went to see her during the time she was in hospital. I suspect they conducted their affair just as they always had, in the wards, in secret places. The copse in the grounds was quite thick, she once told me, smiling to herself.

Poor Gregory died early, developing lumps just like his dog Bob, his body riddled with cancer. My father divorced my mother, and she never loved anyone again but Gregory, and stayed loyal to his memory. Eventually, she was released from the hospital, and once I had my own home, she came to live with me, because I owed her that for the agony I had caused her.

There are other people now in Crowsley Beck, a new family at The Farings. I went back recently for the first time in my adult life. It was smarter, paint-shinier, richer, the ideal commuter village, though the railway station had closed decades before. The *power station had been decommissioned, and Ragdell Place turned into a hotel. After years of neglect, Brinden had been taken over by developers as its notoriety gradually faded. I didn't want to look at it; I didn't want to spoil the memory of that summer when it was my playground, or think of Jennifer there, obediently holding flowers.*

Children ran across the shining grass, beeches replacing the elms, the pond ringed with a fence. There were blinds, not curtains, at The Farings, and the outer wall that faced the green seemed to bulge faintly, the bricks compacted and undulating. Children's voices emerged from inside the house; a cat that looked somewhat like Meribell sat on the wall, and scales were played with amateur force on a piano. As I left, I looked up at the tiny window of the room in the roof, and the sun caught it in its emptiness.

Je Reviens.

AFTERWORD

I spent my first years in the village of the damned.

This was the picture postcard idyll that is Letchmore Heath in Hertfordshire, just north of London, which was the location for the celebrated 1960 film based on John Wyndham's novel *The Midwich Cuckoos*. *Village of the Damned* features a colony of demonic blond children terrorising the law-abiding residents of a sleepy village. It was here I spent my first four years, the place preserved for me in a series of detailed memories that possess an almost hyper-real clarity.

I never revisited it until last year, when my son was invited to a bar mitzvah in nearby Radlett. I was curious, and we decided to drive through the village on the way back.

There it was. It was like a dream made real, a memory rolling out in front of me in brilliant colour, more polished and privileged than it had been, but so exactly as I had remembered it, I could find my way to certain houses without hesitation and recall the layout of the two cottages in which we had lived. A skylight featured in my memory, as did the pattern of wallpaper up close, the texture of tiles: that microscopic vision, only possible for a very young child in its small world, was burned into my mind with what turned out to be quite disquieting accuracy.

When Random House approached me to write a Hammer novella, this shimmering archetypal English village leapt into my mind immediately as the setting. That, and a girl dressed in Victorian clothes on a green, were my starting points. Was it because of the famed film? I don't think so, though that may have overlaid my memories and enhanced my decision to set the novella in the early 1960s; and I'm sure that something of the Midwich children's stares ended up in the blank gaze of Jennifer Crale. It was more a sense that perfection can be eerie. Beneath the grass-bright surface of such prettiness there had to be more going on: it seemed to me that the quiet margins of such a place and a time would foster unease. I spent my later childhood in a more obviously haunted house in the middle of a moor, but it was this tight little village that suggested ghosts to me, and so my Crowsley Beck was born.

In 1963, parochial England was still muffled in a time warp, little changed since the fifties. The Swinging Sixties had yet to take hold. While the new decade was beginning to explode elsewhere, it would only just have been starting to spread its tendrils into the quaint cluster of pensioners and churchgoers, of sewing circles and obedient children that formed a village such as Letchmore Heath. Kennedy was still alive that summer; the moon was still virgin territory; fashion, music and casual sex were happening, but not for married women. In that tension between different eras, between women's status and their suppressed desires, lay much that was simmering, seething and capable of transforming anger or despair into mental distortion.

Ghosts don't sit easily with our vision of that decade, and I liked the idea of setting Victorians – a real one, and an odd, aspiring one – there among the bright home-knits and mown grass. Crowsley Beck uses the very heart of the village of my infancy, and then invention takes over. There was no Brinden there, though shades of that house once existed else-where; naturally, no nuclear power station was ever built so close to London; no cottages that I knew were knocked through, and nor was there a school for disabled children, though the aerodrome and the psychiatric hospital existed.

All my novels are haunted, but until I was asked to write *Touched*, I didn't realise this. One way or another my characters are haunted by their pasts, their mistakes, their longings; pursued by guilt and desire so strong, it could infiltrate a life. If you make that haunting manifest, there is much to experiment with, and playing with the conventions of the ghost and horror story affords a strange sort of pleasure. Houses in rebellion, secret rooms, figures glimpsed obliquely, unexplained smells are here juxtaposed with more earthly horror. I wanted the discomfiting, downright dodgy element of the Pollards in my story so that live humans coincide with more benign presences, the living wreaking more damage than the restless dead. I wanted to explore love so determined it goes rotten, poor Evangeline unable to move beyond her identification with her grandmother; I wanted to find haunting where characters don't expect it, while they're looking elsewhere.

I wrote this novella with an urgency and intensity that was a release after the agonies of creating a longer novel. Strangely, I did something I had never done before as a writer: I saw the plot in almost complete form, perceiving the structure, the time frame and the characters simultaneously, and I sat there in a frenzy of invention one afternoon in the British Library. It was only Freddie, the lost child, who – appropriately enough – came in later, starting out as an imaginary friend of Eva's but taking on an independent life and past.

The supernatural or paranormal comes into its own in film and shorter fiction. There are very few full-length ghost novels, the short story or novella allowing a suspension of disbelief that would be strained by a longer work. The novella seems the perfect length for a ghost tale, and the greatest of all, *The Turn of the Screw*, is only around forty-three thousand words long.

I had always liked the Gothic, the dark, disconcerting and somewhat unsavoury in literature. It's the glimpse of the intangible that intrigues me; the almost-thereness, the glimmer of awareness of another presence, or the stain of an emotion, just beyond our normal comprehension. Giving free rein to what might lie in the shadows taunts and tantalises, and in strange ways liberates the writer to move into unexplored realms. As a reader, I love to be disturbed. In *Touched*, I wanted the darkness in the brightness to spring to life.

Joanna Briscoe, 2014

ALSO AVAILABLE FROM HAMMER

Breakfast with the Borgias
DBC Pierre

'Hell is other people.' A chilling, page-turning Hammer novella by DBC Pierre, the Booker-Prize-winning author of *Vernon God Little*.

The setting: a faded, lonely guesthouse on the Suffolk coast. Outside, it's dark and very foggy. Inside, there's no phone or internet reception, no hope of connectivity with the outside world.

Enter Ariel Panck, a promising young academic en route from the USA to a convention in Amsterdam. With his plane grounded at Stansted, he has been booked in for the night at the guesthouse.

Discombobulated and jetlagged, he falls in with a family who appear to be commemorating an event.

But this is no ordinary commemoration. And this is no ordinary family.

As evening becomes night, Panek realises that he has become caught in an insidious web of other people's secrets and lies, a Sartrian hell from which there may be for him no escape . . .

'If any novelist can collate the killing irony of what is happening around us, it is DBC Pierre'
Guardian

About Hammer

Hammer is the most well-known film brand in the UK, having made over 150 feature films which have been terrifying and thrilling audiences worldwide for generations.

Whilst synonymous with horror and the genre-defining classics it produced in the 1950s to 1970s, Hammer was recently rebooted in the film world as the home of "Smart Horror", with the critically acclaimed *Let Me In* and *The Woman in Black*. With *The Woman in Black: Angel of Death* scheduled for 2014, Hammer has been re-born.

Hammer's literary legacy is also now being revived through its new partnership with Arrow Books. This series features original novellas by some of today's most celebrated authors, as well as classic stories from nearly a century of production.

In 2014 Hammer Arrow will publish books by DBC Pierre, Lynne Truss and Joanna Briscoe as well as a novelisation of the forthcoming *The Woman in Black: Angel of Death*, continuing a programme that began with bestselling novellas from Helen Dunmore and Jeanette Winterson. Beautifully produced and written to read in a single sitting, Hammer Arrow books are perfect for readers of quality contemporary fiction.

For more information on Hammer
visit: www.hammerfilms.com or
www.facebook.com/hammerfilms